STOLEN STAR

The arrival of a wealthy family of French settlers in Sunset County, Arizona, put a strain upon the forces of law and order, and also affected Mike Liddell, troubleshooter to Madeleine la Baronne de Beauclerc. At a fancy dress reception, property was mislaid. To get close to the suspects, Mike allowed himself to be locked up with them — and so his troubles started. Meanwhile, a new, lethal enemy of law and order, as well as the Beauclerc outfit, menaced the County . . .

Books by David Bingley
in the Linford Western Library:

THE BEAUCLERC BRAND
ROGUE'S REMITTANCE

DAVID BINGLEY

STOLEN STAR

Complete and Unabridged

LINFORD
Leicester

First published in Great Britain in 2000
under the name of 'David Horsley'

First Linford Edition
published 2002

British Library CIP Data

Bingley, David, *1920* –
　　Stolen star.—Large print ed.—
　　Linford western library
　　1. Western stories
　　2. Large type books
　　I. Title
　　823.9'14 [F]

　　ISBN 0–7089–9915–8

Published by
F. A. Thorpe (Publishing)
Anstey, Leicestershire

Set by Words & Graphics Ltd.
Anstey, Leicestershire
Printed and bound in Great Britain by
T. J. International Ltd., Padstow, Cornwall
This book is printed on acid-free paper

1

In an isolated valley to the west of Sunset County, New Mexico territory, four white Americans were toiling through the latter hours of an early summer's morning to rebuild the shattered husk of a roomy log cabin.

Some ten years earlier, the original family had used the building as the headquarters of a stagecoach relay station. More recently, a trio who did not seek the public eye had taken it over. Earl Marden and his two sidekicks had once made a living riding the trails as renegades. Now, they were a respectable firm of undertakers, working when they needed to and only using their skills with firearms for the benefit of their friends.

Nevertheless, they were always watchful.

Above the flat roof, and housed in a central turret, Earl Marden himself was going through the motions of panning a newly assembled Gatling gun which commanded a wide view of the approach meadow on the gentle slope opposite. Quite a useful distance away, moving from one extremity of vision to the other, was a tall handsome muscular character who walked with an easy grace. Michael Bonnard Liddell was in his middle twenties. Stripped to the waist, his chest and back showed as much sunburn as his full clean-shaven face.

From the turret, Marden called hoarsely. 'Move a bit further to your right, Mike. I can still get you in line!'

About thirty yards away to the walker's left, the Bayer brothers, Rusty and Sam, paused in their labours with a long heavy two-handled saw. Sam, the younger of the two, was down in a shallow pit, out of sight except from the turret. Rusty, in the upper position, breathed noisily through his small tight mouth and inwardly curved nose. As his breathing eased, he absently

2

scratched the sandy mat of hair on his chest.

'Hey, Earl, when are we goin' to break for coffee?' Rusty queried huskily.

'Yer, that goes for me, too, Boss!' Sam's voice was muted by the pit walls, but there was no mistaking his needs. 'Down here in this bear pit is hotter than hell, so give us a bit of encouragement, why don't you?'

To show his approval of the Bayers' suggestions, Mike Liddell came to a halt and seated himself on the grass, cross-legged.

Marden straightened up with exaggerated frustration showing in his gesture. 'All right, all right, gang up on me then. See if I care!' He paced around the small platform where the gun was housed a couple of times. 'Will you believe I can smell the coffee right up here? So take a break. Come on indoors!'

All at once the reluctant workers developed energy. Rusty helped Sam out of the pit. Mike rose to his feet and plodded down the meadow. Marden disappeared from sight, on his way to the stove in the kitchen. Mike reached the front gallery first. He waited for the brothers.

'What time was that carter fellow supposed to bring the planks out from Indian Ridge?'

'Before noon,' Sam answered. He talked noisily through his nose which had been flattened in a fight at an early age. 'He promised. Soon, he'll be late. Maybe the smell of the coffee will speed him up.'

The four men assembled in the partially furnished kitchen of the house, seated themselves on stools and took a mug of coffee each. Mike went looking for his shirt and came back with four small cigars, which he handed round. From time to time, they gazed around them, as if recalling that earlier time when an enemy had used an older gatling gun against them as they approached the building.

Five minutes later, the familiar

sounds of a heavy cart on the move drifted in through a window space which lacked glass. Without showing an excess of interest they shifted across to the nearest window on the east side and casually watched the long battered open cart roll towards them, pulled by two mules.

Will Gates, a bow-legged, freckled, stooping farmer with a lined face was gripping the reins as if he was controlling a chariot team. Beside him was his younger son, Geordie, a lad of thirteen: growing out of his cutdown pants and scratching a chin which had never known a razor. Geordie was the first to react. As soon as he saw the faces, he lifted his feathered straw hat and waved it, revealing carrotty unshorn hair unused to a brush.

Earl remarked: 'I don't figure that young fellow will spend all his days as a dirt farmer. What do you say?'

The discussion had not developed very far when the lad sprinted up to the back door and knocked on it, entering without waiting for a reply.

'We got your planks, Mr Marden. Mr Martin, that is. An' I've brought a special letter from the French lady for Mr Liddell. Here you are, Mike!'

The boy's soiled hands had left a couple of grubby marks on the envelope, but Mike overlooked that and grinned and expressed his thanks. Earl directed the father and son to the nearby shed, where the planks were to be stored, while Mike excused himself and moved into another room to read his letter. It was written in the pleasantly-rounded hand of Madame de Beauclerc, herself.

Chateau Beauclerc,
Tuesday.

Mon cher Michel,

I am so pleased to know that the restoration of our dear friend Earl's home is nearing completion.

The terrible conflict which almost devastated the whole edifice is still too vivid, too horrific to think of. Thank God we didn't have any further casualties.

Mollie, Carmelita and Joseph are all well and send you their love. (Joseph's back is troubling him a little, but he won't let us talk about it.)

Alas, I am running a slight fever, which will prevent me from attending the planned reception party of our new French neighbours in Riverside, the Duponts. Monsieur Dupont, I believe, is a wealthy banker from the south of France who retired early and came over to the U.S. of A. on account of his wife's delicate chest.

By the way, our precocious little friend, Isabella, will be there. She is to play her violin in the small orchestra. Pierre, the Duponts' bachelor son, plays the cello. Perhaps the Duponts will be matchmaking as Pierre has so far failed to find the right sort of marriage partner in mainland France.

Now, to business, dear Michel. You don't need to be reminded of the valuable artifacts which I have loaned to the Duponts from the chateau, here, and also from the late Gerda Lehmann's magnificent shop, in Middleton. I want you to go to the reception yourself to keep an eye on our properties, and also on little Isabella, of course.

I am enclosing my own invitation. What I have written on the back should facilitate your reception. I close with my warm regards to Earl, Sam and Rusty, and my constant affection for yourself. Don't be out of touch for longer than you can help. My imagination plays tricks when you are away.

Yours sincerely,
Madeleine. X

For over a minute, Mike sank back in the chair with his eyes closed. The unmistakable style of la Baronne's writing had transported him to the atmosphere of the sumptuous dwelling where he lived and worked in Sundown City. Almost, he could smell the expensive, exclusive perfume which Madeleine wore habitually. Her warm cultured personality was there with him in the partially refurbished shack which he was helping to restore.

He was still in that relaxed position, drawing gently on his small cigar when Earl looked in at the door.

'All good news, is it, Mike?'

Mike grinned and encouraged Earl to sit down in the chair opposite. The former outlaw leader was an imposing figure, however he was comporting himself. In his early forties, he was six-feet two-inches tall, a well distributed thirteen stones in weight and he walked with a controlled muscular roll. His sandy hair was trimmed short, revealing grey highlights which matched the touches of grey in his sideburns. At times, his neutral-coloured eyes could appear like gimlets on either side of the strong Roman nose. His skin, though leathery, looked healthy.

'Madeleine is running a slight fever which will prevent her from goin' to the house-warmin' party at the Riverside place. The Duponts, they're called. She's asked me to get over there to keep an eye on some valuables she's loaned from the chateau and the Lehmann house, an' keep tabs on that wayward little sweetie from the Alvarez place. Isabella. So I think I'll push off when I've checked over my horses, if you don't mind, Earl.'

Marden grunted, nodded and grinned. 'It's nice to know she doesn't need a hearse, or a team of protectors with shootin' irons. Especially at a time like this when we're given over to house buildin'. I take it you'll keep in touch, though. Watch the lines of communications, eh?'

Mike chuckled. He agreed. They rose together and ambled out of the room with their hands resting on one another's shoulders.

Fifteen minutes later, Mike swung

into the saddle of his chestnut, ready to ride out. Also with him was the young farmer's son, Geordie Gates. The lad had helped to saddle the chestnut, and then he had asked permission to ride a little way with Mike on the back of the second horse, a palomino, which was sporting a small pack saddle.

Earl, the Bayers and Will Gates stood in a group, encroaching as they said their farewells. Mike promised to start Geordie on the way back within a half mile. The lad looked precociously cheerful behind the pale horse's pack saddle. His expression seemed to suggest that he would ride a lot further than half a mile.

Soon, the two riders were up the slope fronting on the relay station and about to crest the hill and drop down the other side. Mike rose up in his stirrups, called his last farewell and added one or two Spanish phrases of a friendly nature, and then they were out of sight.

On the downgrade, Geordie pulled

11

out a mouth organ and played a few
martial tunes with a lot of wind and an
excess of vamping. Mike, however, was
in a thoughtful mood and unresponsive.

Geordie called: 'Hey, Mike I heard
tell that killer fellow used a swivel
holster against you, back there at Earl's
place! Does it give a gunman a lot of
advantage?'

'Certainly, it does,' Mike called back
curtly. 'It's a killer's gun! You don't
want to bother your mind about that
sort of hardware!'

Mike's brusque manner curtailed the
lad's rush of enthusiasm, but when the
troubleshooter was doing an almost
unconscious check of his own weapons,
something akin to hero worship began
to bubble up again in the youngster's
mind.

'Know what I'd like more than
anything, right now, Mike?'

'All right, Geordie, what is it?
Something to do with Samuel Colt,
eh?' Mike turned and glared at him.
'Well, I was figurin' to exercise my

essential weapons after you headed back towards your Pa, but if it will serve to stop you shooting off your mouth, I'll give it a go now!'

Geordie lifted his hat, gave his well-thatched crown a good scratching, thought of one or two encouraging answers and, at the last moment, decided to remain silent. He did the right thing.

Mike studied a series of upthrust rocks siding the beginnings of an ill-marked trail. He scowled, looked around for better targets, failed to find any, and adjusted himself in the saddle. A quiet nudge here and there was meant to warn the chestnut that he was about to make some noise.

He pulled his right-handed Colt quite smoothly. However, it did not appear to clear leather with sufficient speed. So, he holstered it again, and worked on his draw. After five or six efficient efforts, he felt satisfied. The next one was followed up immediately by a series of shots at six trailside rocks, all in sequence. The shooting was over in a very short time. Dust and stone chippings filled the air. All animal life had discreetly departed. At the first shot, the chestnut had flinched, which made the bullet hit the first stone lower than was intended. It changed direction at a big acute angle and buzzed into nearby mesquite. All the other bullets hit the extreme top of the rocks and merely flaked off a small amount of chippings.

Geordie whistled, but Mike ignored him. With his gauntlets between his teeth he thumbed more bullets from his gun belt into the empty chambers with casual dexterity. Even reloading was an essential skill to a troubleshooter. Next, he repeated the operation on the left side. It involved swinging the Colt across the neck of the horse, but the aiming remained good and the animal did nothing to affect the result.

For a minute or two, the palomino in the rear pranced about. Geordie struggled to get it under control without asking for advice. It took him all the time Mike needed to practise bringing his Winchester clear of the saddle scabbard, and get it up to his shoulder. He fired three shots to his left, easily removing twigs from trees at a fair distance, but the other three, which called for a swivelling in the saddle to aim on the right side, were not loosened off quite so quickly.

'Hey, Mike, I'm learnin' things, watchin' you! If I was your enemy, I'd be on your right side an' wide of the trail. Does that sound like good reasonin'?'

'Yer, but I'm not seekin' to teach you anything about guns, young fellow. A safer place is totally out of range.'

As the Winchester .73 was restored, loaded, to the scabbard, Geordie Gates rocked with laughter: so much so that he almost fell out of the saddle. Mike turned to face him, distracted.

'What's botherin' you, son?'

Geordie coughed, cleared his throat, and pointed an index finger at his questioner. 'You, Mike! You're one hell of a leg puller, I guess. All this time you've been teasin' me about my interest in guns, an' you, you're absolutely captivated by 'em yourself!'

'Shut up an' come here!' Mike yelled. Geordie hastily complied.

'When you grow up, lad, don't seek a trade which depends upon guns! Don't live by the bullet. Killin' is a mean trade, even if you're workin' against enemies of society! I only do it because I'm committed to safeguardin' people weaker than myself — an' their property!

'I'd like you to understand that bullets curtailed the lives of two of my brothers, in the big war. An' my father, a doctor, also died of wounds. So you'll realise why I'm not exactly in favour of livin' by the gun. It isn't healthy!'

Mike had spoken with such ferocity that Geordie overreacted, lost his balance and fell on his back in the dust. At once, he recovered his dislodged hat, stuck it on his head and prepared to run back along the trail.

'Hold it! Give me the reins before you run off!'

Mike indulged in a few deep breaths to ease the anger which had built up in him. He took the proffered reins, gestured with his hand to indicate a handshake and left a silver dollar in the boy's palm. The lad started to shake his head, and then thought better of it.

'Sorry, Mike, I didn't know about your brothers an' that! Have a good trip, why don't you?'

'I shouldn't have sounded off at you, Geordie. One thing more, don't be in too big a hurry to grow up. Bein' a growing lad has a lot goin' for it. *Adios*!'

The boy ran fifty yards, seated himself on a boulder and watched the rider and horses slowly become indistinct, due to distance and dust.

2

Riverside, a comparatively new settlement in the county of Sunset, was more than an ordinary day's ride away from Earl Marden's remote dwelling. However, the Dupont invitation made it clear that Mike had a night in hand before he needed to be in touch with the newcomers beside the Pecos River.

This suited Mike's itinerary as he had business to conduct in Middleton, a more mature town some five miles west. He rode the chestnut at a smooth, economic pace and found himself plodding through Middleton shortly after two o'clock in the afternoon.

There was little sign of business activity at that hour of the afternoon. For the siesta, some had retired to bed. Others lolled in the shade afforded by galleries and sidewalks.

The bric a brac shop which had

belonged to the late Gerda Lehmann had plenty of valuable gear on view, but the shop door was locked and a notice advised any enquirer to call at the house next door, occupied by the Wakeford family.

Mike could have done that, but his business was personal and he wanted to make contact with Eleonora May Rondell, the granddaughter of Charlton Wagner, the local bank president. Ellie May was only twenty years of age; a lithe, sparely built beauty with long plaited brown tresses and the keen blue eyes of an artist in oils. Due to her interest in all things artistic, Ellie May had taken over a lot of the running of the shop, which sold — among other valuables — oil paintings and an occasional water colour.

The young Texan knew where to find Ellie May, if she was in town. She would be in her quarters at the hacienda of her grandfather, the banker. The heat and dust had sapped a lot of the rider's energy, but as he rode out towards the banker's residence, a sound floated out to meet him which made it all sound worthwhile.

The medieval tune, Greensleeves, sensitively played upon a flute carried across the still sultry air from the open windows of the upper room of the spacious Spanish style building.

Mike negotiated the five-barred gate, eased the led horse through it and angled his quadrupeds towards the hitchrail fronting the house. As he did so, he licked his dry lips, summoned up a few deep breaths and whistled in accompaniment with the flautist's efforts. He found the effort tiring, in the heat of the afternoon. He hummed a few bars, sung as much of the words as he could remember and suddenly gave up.

'Hola! Eleonora!'

The music stopped. Briefly, Eleonora glanced out of her window. Her blue eyes rounded with suppressed delight. She dropped out of sight, chuckling to herself.

'Who calls the lady in her boudoir?'

'Sir Michael, protector of the French chateau! Are you dressed, presentable and in a receptive mood, for my business is urgent!'

'All right, Michael, come on up. I'm tired of my music lesson, anyway, and I have business with you, too.'

Before the newcomer could enter the house, a young negro boy raced across from the stable, intent upon making off with the two horses. Mike greeted him, intimated that his stay would be a short one, and then left him to lightly groom the animals and take them into the shade. In the hallway, the young Texan bent down and removed his boots.

From above, Ellie May whispered: 'Keep your stetson on, amigo.'

Mike frowned to himself, and then grinned. Two minutes later, he padded into the girl's extensive living quarters with paint-daubed easels adjacent to two big dormer-type windows. The girl was hiding behind the second of the two. She sprang into view, barefooted, and lightly gripped him about the waist, from the rear.

'Hey, Ellie, what in tarnation are you up to?' Mike grumbled mildly. 'an' what's this business you have with me?'

The girl allowed him to free himself, although she did little to assist him. When they were face to face and sharing a light embrace, Ellie said: 'Michael, I want to capture your features forever! Is that a compliment, do you think?'

Although he was aware of the dust and perspiration which had accrued during his ride, Mike nevertheless, raised her from the ground and kissed her rather warmly. Ellie flushed a little, blinked several times, and returned Mike's ardour.

'Ellie, love, the heat has been workin' on me. Don't ask questions which need a lot of thought, eh? So I kissed you with my hat on. Now, what was it about keepin' on my stetson?'

The girl moved easily in her light buckskin tunic. She released his neck from her gentle clutch, and dabbed him with his bandanna about the head.

'I've been looking forward to a visit from you for ages, Mike. Now you're here, I feel I could ask you questions for hours and hours. We've always been close, always. So you won't mind me asking personal questions. Here's a beauty. If you had decided to change your ways, in favour of marriage, what sort of a woman would you choose to share your life with you?'

At once she darted away from him, ran to a table and poured out a tall glass of cool fruit cordial. She came back with it and presented it to him. Mike had chuckled at first, but one close glance at the dimpled finely-chiselled serious face made him take the matter seriously.

'My, my, little squaw, the answer might be a little embarrassing. Give me a few seconds to collect my thoughts, will you?'

He drank some of the cordial, moved

around the room and casually uncovered the first of the two canvases. He whistled, as he pored over a fine study of Maria, the Wagner housekeeper, toiling to raise water from a well in the yard. He glanced sharply at the girl, wondering how much pleasure she had derived from the painting. Ellie was nervously tugging at her two long brown plaits and shifting from one foot to the other.

'You have exceptional talent, Ellie. I'm proud to know you.'

'Thank you, Sir Michael. But I would like an answer to my question, if you please.'

In order to avoid his probing eyes, she moved away to a bench, where her painting materials lay and selected a brush. Presently, her nimble fingers were mixing colour in a palette. Her restlessness communicated itself to Mike, who danced across to the other easel, stood behind it with his glass of cordial, and eased away the second cover. His height made it possible for him to regard her with just his head above the canvas.

'Well Mr Troubleshooter?'

Mike half closed his eyes. 'I'd choose a woman who was capable of thinking beyond the ordinary bounds of society, beyond the western frontier, if you like. A female with creative talent would suit me. Like a painter, who sometimes could see with the eyes of an owl, and then with the eyes of an eagle. She would have sensitive ears, too. So, I guess it would help if she could appreciate music, play an instrument.'

Suddenly, Mike realised that he was giving a description of a woman which would fit his listener. He gasped, opened his eyes wide and then gasped again, as he saw the look of intense annoyance which his words had produced.

Holding in her fury, Ellie leapt across the room with a jar of dirty paint brush water in her hand, intent upon hurling the liquid at the painting on the canvas which Mike had still not seen. Perceiving what she intended to do, he rounded the easel from behind and spread himself to protect the canvas from the paint water which was bound to ruin it.

Uncertainty flickered behind the girl's blue eyes, but she was too far advanced in her movement to hold back at that stage. The contents of the jar splashed across Mike's shirt, his face and his stetson. Ellie pulled up like a statue, except that her breast was heaving under the tunic which draped her upper body.

Mike blinked the water out of his eyes. 'So that's why I had to keep my stetson on,' he commented very calmly.

Ellie stepped away, uncertainly. 'I, er, I'm sorry, but you shouldn't have teased me. After all, I *am* a woman in years. I'll be twenty-one in a few months' time! I was serious when I asked you the question!'

Mike whipped off his hat, and then his shirt. He wiped off his face and threw the shirt aside. 'I, too, was absolutely serious, Ellie. It didn't occur to me until I had said it all that you had, you have all the attributes!'

He turned away, to hide the depths of his embarrassment. And then he saw the second painting. He knew at once that it was special. It portrayed a typical outdoor western character, standing in the stirrups of a stationary horse, and staring forward at some distant object. In his two hands was a spyglass. He was in the act of bringing up the glass to his face.

All the detail was there, every crack and fissure of the rocky outcrop on which the horse and rider rested. The horse was finely drawn. After studying it for a mere few seconds, Mike knew a lot more about Ellie's sensitive emotional state. The horse was his own palomino, and the figure portrayed tall in the saddle was none other than himself. He knew it instinctively, even though the face was an indistinct blur of light colour wash. Ellie wanted him

27

there in person, wearing his hat, so that she could put in the details at first hand.

'Forgive me, Ellie, and do go on with what you had planned. There's a tube of paper over there. If I grip that and simulate the expression you want, everything will be all right. Come along now, no tears. You've captured me in oils, on canvas an' I'm proud of that. Why, it puts me on a par with that other boy friend of yours, Johnnie Two Feathers, doesn't it?'

Johnnie Two Feathers was on the payroll of Charlton Wagner, Ellie's banker grandfather. He had acted as Ellie's protector on many occasions. Johnnie's likeness in full war paint hung in the hall of the house.

Mike groaned. He embraced Ellie with a show of gentleness. 'I'm bein' facetious at the wrong time, unintentionally. Sorry, my dear. Now, finish mixin' your paint, will you, otherwise I won't be able to concentrate on my posing. Will it do if I stand over towards the other easel, or do you want me nearer?'

The girl was slow to slip away from his embrace and give her attention to the job in hand. Mike kept his thoughts to himself as she directed him to the best spot for the job. He was thinking that a capable artist who knew her subject well ought to be able to reproduce a familiar expression without benefit of the model. However, he did not raise any more queries, and the girl was soon sufficiently in control of herself to rough in the features, and follow up with detail.

Presently, his fingers grew tired. He asked permission to move. When it was granted he crossed the floor and picked up the flute, using it as a substitute for the paper cylinder. Ellie stopped licking her lips with the tip of her tongue and smiled winningly.

'By the way, Ellie, I hope you're going to the Duponts. There'll be an opportunity to join in with the small orchestra there. Play alongside of

Didier Dupont, who is a cellist, and Isabel Valero, whom you already know.'

'I'm not going, Michael,' Ellie replied firmly. 'My music is not good enough, and I don't have the wit to go into that kind of gathering!'

Mike's expression hardened with disappointment. 'Hell, I was looking forward to your company, Ellie. Are you sure you won't change your mind? This is a fine opportunity to pick up a few dance steps, to dress up and make conversation — '

'I'm not that sort of person, Mike. At least, not yet. Now, if we could change the topic of conversation. All the guests have to wear fancy dress. I wanted to talk to you about yours. There are several outfits at the Lehmann store which would fit you for the occasion. If you want my advice, think seriously about the bull fighter's outfit. There's the hat, the cummerbund, special trousers and a neat short jacket. Besides, we can provide a cape if you want it, and a real toreador's sword!'

The discussion went on for a short while. Several of the available costumes would have altered Mike's image altogether. A Venetian gondolier, for instance, or a Chinese coolie. Ellie gave grudging consideration to the outfit of a South American gaucho, but she really thought it was not sufficiently at variance with the everyday gear of a North American cowpuncher. Mike perceived this, and he had almost made up his mind by the time the intense young artist had finished putting in the facial details. By that time, Ellie had become very sweet again. She produced for her visitor a light salad lunch and patiently waited for him to eat it before taking him along to town, and in particular to the Lehmann store which she managed, along with others.

Cut glass mobiles tinkled gently in the light breeze as Ellie unlocked the door. Mike peered around at the wonderland of trinkets, baubles, curios and expensive items of furniture.

'Go through to the front room,

upstairs,' Ellie remarked. 'Let's get the fitting over an' then you can take a bath, or have a late siesta on the back gallery. How will that suit you?'

'You're the boss, Ellie. I'm in your hands.'

★   ★   ★

The complete outfit of the toreador was almost a perfect fit. Mike accepted it without demur. It gave him a rakish look, made him want to use an arrogant expression to go with it, and it certainly put an added twinkle into the blue eyes of his artistic admirer.

Ellie raised her arms and went through a few steps of a paso doble. She was pleased when Mike adopted a toreador's stance, but very shortly afterwards she curtailed the action due to the calculating look in the back of his eyes.

'You'll do very well as a bull fighter. Just be careful about the sword, though. It's quite sharp. If you have to, play

32

around with the cape. Give the sharp steel a miss. Me, I'm goin' to see grandfather at the dinero emporium. Do you need to draw any money?'

'If you'll be so kind, little squaw, I could use one hundred dollars from the Beauclerc general account. Don't be away too long. I'll bathe and sleep, an' man the counter if anyone gets too impatient. If only you'd change your mind and come with me to Riverside, Ellie. You could tint your face, an' rub a few mint leaves over your body for perfume, and go as an Indian princess. How does that sound to you?'

Ellie paused in the doorway and shot him a long thoughtful look.

'Not that you require any perfume, little squaw. There I go, talkin' carelessly again!'

'I shall not be goin' with you, amigo, but that was a nice try. Don't forget you're goin' on duty. Besides, I'd cramp your style, wouldn't I?'

Mike danced after her, but she was gone: down the stairs and round the counter. Pursuit was hopeless. He returned to the upper floor, stared hard at the large European bath intended for sale. It was kept topped up with cool water on account of a prospective buyer having asked to try it. As soon as the shop door had closed finally, Mike gave way to tiredness again. All the time he was stripping off for his bath, he was studying the intriguing shelf where the bath salts were kept.

★　★　★

The first thing that Mike noticed as he roused himself from his sleeping position on the bench under the back awning of the building was a change in the position of the sun. It had shifted quite considerably across towards the west since he dragged himself out of the bath and gave himself over to siesta.

Someone tinkled the bell in the shop, which meant a customer was in there. The young troubleshooter blinked hard, wondering if he should be in the shop, manning the counter as he had promised. He strained to hear an exchange of words. The customer was female, and the assistant had a slightly immature male voice which still had a trace of an English accent. Recognising it, Mike grinned to himself and settled back again to rest a while longer.

Young Harry Wakeford had been useful to him before. He was small and bright and often wore a sailor's suit and lace-up boots, due to his mother's somewhat eccentric habits. However, the woman saw to her son's education and as she was gifted herself, he took no harm in that direction. Having effected a sale, Harry stepped out at the back, cleared his throat gently and beamed when Mike showed that he was awake.

'So nice to see you again, Michael,' he remarked earnestly. 'I'm in charge at the moment. What a lot has happened since we first met. Miss Lehmann shot to death, and you yourself temporarily in difficulties due to the actions of her associates.'

'Nice to see you again, Harry. But don't dwell on the past. You're still being useful about the place. You've lost Gerda, but gained Ellie in a manner of speaking. Now, what's that list you're clutching so purposefully? Is it for me?'

Harry nervously finger-combed his fair curls and handed over the paper. It was a list of items loaned from the store to the Duponts, for display purposes, at the coming reception. Four miniatures, two silver salvers, silver sauce boats, hand-carved jade figurines, Japanese fans and many trinkets. Mike whistled.

'Hey, this is some list. Let's hope we don't get any light-fingered guests at the Dupont residence!'

He glanced up sharply to study Harry's reaction to his words, and noted that the anguished, troubled look was still lurking on the boy's plump face.

'What is it, Harry? If you're in trouble you've only got to say so.'

The lad glanced through to the shop, making sure that it was empty. He then closed the communicating door and seated himself beside Mike, who had risen as far as a sitting position.

'I may have done something rather foolish, Michael. When I'm at liberty, I often slip along the High Street and sit near the saloons. Not inside, you understand. But near, so that I can hear what the cowmen and ranchers and prospectors are saying. Sometimes they tease me about the way I'm dressed, but I find them awfully interesting.

'Well, there was a group who seemed to have been drinkin' slowly for quite a long time. They were sleepy. Just when I thought one of them was dozing off, another fellow pulled some cards from his pocket, blinked himself alert again, and tried to conjure with them. Only his hands were unsteady, and when he bent them and tried to flick them from one hand to the other, he failed to catch them and they went all over the floor. I picked a couple up for him. That's how I know what they were!'

'And what in fact were they, Harry?

Mike asked curiously.

'Invitation cards for the Dupont reception, Mike, and they didn't look the type, at all. I mean, they were a bit scruffy, you know. Ordinary cow hands, not properly shaved, with trail dust on their clothes and that sort of thing! The first chap said they were invitations to a party, but one of his friends asked me personally if I knew anyone of that name!

'Well, like a fool, I blurted out my knowledge, didn't I? I explained that they were a rich French family just settled in Riverside and I exaggerated the lavishness of the opening reception. Gradually, they stopped fooling around and listened most carefully. It was not until some time later that I realised what I had done. What can I do to put things right, Mike?'

'Are you certain they were genuine Dupont invitation cards, lad?'

'Oh, yes, they were just like the four which we received in the shop. All nicely printed, but without having the guests' named written on them. Mr Wagner received our four, and he put them in the shop for Ellie to use, or dispose of. We've still got ours, so if they were stolen, it wasn't from our shop. That's one good thing, isn't it?'

'They were bound to find out about the reception, even if you hadn't told them, Harry, so don't take on so much guilt. Now, can you describe them? The group with the tickets, I mean.'

Harry nodded. 'A big sharp-faced individual who liked to make marks on chairs with his spur wheels. The man who held them was short, stocky and plump, with a walrus moustache. The gambler type, the one with the short trimmed black moustache and pointed sideburns, he was the one who said they only had to inscribe their names on the cards to be sure of getting in. The fourth one was a quiet type. He walked with a slight roll, not the sort that sailors get. Possibly on account of his being well muscled.'

Mike asked a few more questions,

but Harry did not have a lot more to tell. They strolled back into the shop, came to a halt behind the counter and studied the cards which were in the drawer.

'It could mean trouble for the Duponts, if gate crashers get into their house, Harry, but you shouldn't worry. I'm going along there to keep an eye on Beauclerc interests and the stuff sent along from here. I'm honour bound to do what I can to protect the Duponts, as well.'

The young Texan soon became restless. He left the capable lad in charge and strolled the town, working the public places, looking for the four men who were planning to gate crash the Dupont residence.

In the last of four saloons, a sharp-eyed mean-looking character with a broken stetson brim, took exception to the way in which Mike was examining faces. Liquor had altered the colour of the drinker's eyes. He stepped away from the bar, and swayed a little, waving the beer glass like a weapon.

'Hey, you, hombre! Who do you think you are starin' at folks all the time? *I* think you're some sort of a bounty hunter! What do you say to that?'

Mike grinned and attempted to sidestep him. 'I'd say the beer in here is mighty potent, amigo. Who'd raise a bounty on the likes of you?'

The incident developed instantly. A huge man with a beer gut came hurtling across from the region of the batwings, head down and hat pulled well down. Mike saw the danger signals. Instead of trying to slip his accuser's one handed grip, he put his arms round the fellow's chest, eased him off balance and swung him around so that he faced the menace of the charging giant.

Seconds later, the big man's head collided heavily with the small of his confederate's back. Down went the accuser with a look of agony on his mean features. The charger stumbled to his knees, shaken by the contact with a solid backbone. He removed his crumpled hat, frowned with pain and received a clout beside the head with the beer glass, which Mike had rescued as the other collapsed. Two down and a willing crowd gathering.

Mike handed over the glass to the nearest and keenest and sidestepped his way to the door. Only the swinging batwings marked his departure.

After that, he was observant on two counts. The incident had helped, in a way, by taking some of the tension out of him: but although he searched long and diligently, he failed to locate the original four.

He gave up the search wondering how vulnerable the Duponts would be when a few makeshift renegades got the idea there would be easy pickings.

3

Many of the shops in the new town of Riverside stayed open during the whole of the afternoon on the day of the Duponts' reception. They had flags in the windows, bunting strips across the streets and men dressed up as clowns wearing billboards which proclaimed prosperity brought by Alphonse Dupont, the banker.

Mike Liddell rode in towards the end of siesta time, stabled his palomino, and withdrew for a short rest before presenting himself at the residence and generally getting involved. A meadow at the back of the house served as a parking ground for the rigs and surreys of the visitors. It was also used in part for a minor primitive firework display which preceded everything else.

Mike did another tour, hoping to locate the potential interlopers at the house, but by early evening he was in a remote part of the town, sipping the coolest beer in the township. The crowds were so thick that checking out specific people was practically impossible. The sounds from a small brass band (wages paid by the banker) came from the town square, and it was the oompah music more than anything else which made Mike lose his battle with his conscience and eventually make his way to the big house.

Strolling salesmen plied their trade among folks from town and visitors from the surrounding countryside who had made it a carnival day of sorts. Horsedrawn vehicles negotiated the streets with difficulty. Nearer the house, which was to the south-east of town, the brass band sounds gradually faded. In their place, keen ears were able to detect the sweeter gentler notes of a predominantly string orchestra, coming from the residence itself, the sound escaping through the open ground level windows.

Several extra constables, both white Americans and Mexicans, patrolled the wide approach road with its flanking tall pine-type trees. Mike worked his way through the onlookers, attracted the attention of a mean-looking slow-moving constable and went on to the foot of the front stairs. There, a portly figure with receding sandy hair sported a town marshal's star. He had on a round flat-crowned black hat, a greying dark jacket and striped trousers, and a pearl grey waistcoat. Twin guns looked out of place on him, and yet he had the surly suspicious manner of many middle-aged peace officers in that part of the west.

Flanking the marshal was a stocky deputy, wearing a seafarer's jacket with brass buttons and a big light coloured hat reminiscent of the Confederacy army. Completing the official outdoor trio of reception was a tall thin Frenchman in his middle thirties. Jean-Jacques Perçot had belonged to the banking firm in France. His crisp black hair was parted in the middle; his small moustache was conservatively trimmed. His suit was pearl grey in colour.

'Good evening, gents, I represent Madame la Baronne de Beauclerc, who — as you probably know — is incapacitated. She asked me to come along as her representative. I am Michael Bonnard Liddell.'

Mike outstared the peace officers, who shifted uneasily and glanced significantly in the direction of the young Frenchman. He blinked short-sightedly and hesitated.

Mike prompted him. 'Do you wish your guests to enter by the front door, or another entrance? I ask this because of the fancy dress, you see.'

Perçot acted at if he had seen Mike's holdall for the first time.

'*Bon soir, Monsieur* Liddell. Do you have any means of identification with you? We have to be careful on occasions like these.'

Mike flashed the signet ring with the

46

upraised 'B' in a circle upon it. All three officials were impressed, but slow to react. Consequently, Mike took from his pocket la Baronne's invitation and handed it pointedly to Perçot. This time, there was a reaction. 'If you will come round to the side entrance, *monsieur*.'

Mike followed him. At the side entrance, Perçot murmured 'Pardon' and stepped indoors. Mike replied politely '*Je vous en pris*' and followed him in. The smoothness of the young Texan's French accent took the bank clerk by surprise. Mike was shown into a changing room, which was really an extension of the regular kitchen, curtained off and with battens of extra hooks festooning the walls. Already, upwards of a dozen sets of everyday western trail riding outfits were hung neatly in place.

'If you will be so good as to move towards the sounds of music, when you are ready, I will try and find the opportunity to introduce you to *Monsieur* Dupont and *Madame. A bientôt!*'

Mike grinned at him, and at once began to transform himself into a bull fighter. Although the sounds of stringed instruments and applause came through to him quite strongly, his thoughts were on Ellie May Rondell, her paintings and her concern about his being properly rigged out for this unusual occasion. Madeleine's invitation was placed in his shirt pocket and left there. He figured that the impressive Beauclerc ring would do the trick if anyone else asked for identification.

The house was obviously well built although some of the strained floor-boards creaked. Ahead of him, as he skirted the passages, a dance came to an end amid heavy applause. Someone made an announcement in the silence which followed. He emerged into the main salon and found himself at the back of a crowd. Most of the seats near the floor, and in the alcoves were occupied. Still more people, keen on dancing, stayed on the edges of the floor, awaiting the next dance. A servant brushed past him and lighted a wall lamp, as a rich female voice accompanied only by a piano, began to sing a traditional Spanish love song. He knew the voice, and he smiled, although he was too far back to see the singer.

Isabel Maria Valero. Petite, plump: a honey blonde with grey eyes and an hour glass figure. The heiress to all the possessions of Dona Delfina Emilia Alvarez, a rich Spanish lady assailed in her early seventies by failing health.

In the past year, Isabel's brother — also a musician — had died in tragic circumstances. Isabel herself had been shaken by an unfortunate lover affair with a man who turned out to be a villain. However, there was little sign of sadness in her voice as she trilled her way through the romantic lyrics. As she sang the last verse, the servant who had lighted the lamp touched Mike on the arm and indicated a tray full of facial masks. There were dozens, some small, others larger, all put there for the simple expedient of concealing the upper part of the face from a dancing partner.

Mike thought this extra party convention was an added inducement for thieves to circulate more freely. As the song came to an end, a sudden volume of clapping increased the atmosphere. His pulses quickening, Mike pushed his way forward, his mask in place, as had been requested. His first intention was to cross the dance floor and announce himself to the master and mistress, who were in a recess on the far side slightly to the rear of the dais.

Due to the protracted applause, Isabel came forward without her violin and responded with a low bow. Mike, caught on his way across the floor, whispered an intimate greeting in elided Spanish. The orchestra struck up the opening bars of a paso doble. The girl hesitated between joining the other musicians and stepping down to dance with Michael. The smile he showed beneath his mask helped her to make up her mind.

Several other couples began to go through the intricate rhythms, the twists and turns of the dance meant to portray the antics of a toreador and his cape, but soon the others fell out and many standing watchers clapped the two-step rhythm for the girl and her masked bull fighter. At the end, they bowed and were given a great reception. Isabel was breathless, and Mike felt warm in his unaccustomed suit, but he managed to exchange a few words with his partner before her commitments drew her away.

'Lovely to see you again, Isabel, even if you are taken up with entertaining our new neighbours!'

'*Buenas tardes*, Michael. So glad you could come. I notice la Baronne is missing. You, I suppose, will be on duty, looking after all the ornaments, and the fragile ladies. Whatever you do, don't cross young Monsieur Didier. That's him playing the cello. See, he's glaring at us already. Very formal, very stiff. And prickly with jealousy! *Adios, amigo.*'

'*Hasta la vista*, Isabel.'

Mike was about to move away from the dais, but out of his eye corner he detected the special interest of Madame Dupont, who was ogling him distinctly through her lorgnettes. Acting upon impulse, he bowed from the waist to her and her husband and then moved off, gradually working his way through the dancers towards the windows at the front of the house. His intention was to plant himself beside an open window, light a small cigar and at the same time, survey the guests in an effort to study anything untoward. The partners swaying to waltz rhythm helped him for a time, but then to his surprise the dance appeared to be cut short.

Didier Marcel Dupont, an imposing figure with his pale thin features and high cheekbones, moved around his cello and stepped forward to speak.

'*Messieurs mesdames*, by special request we are about to play a mixing dance. It has different names in different countries. Ladies, if you please, will form a ring and move in a clockwise direction until the music changes. Gentlemen, also in a ring but on the outside, will move in the opposite direction. When the music stops, please choose as a partner the lady nearest in front of you. Until the music changes again . . . '

In order to give the people well away from the dance floor plenty of time to join the more fortunate, the stringed instrument players did a lot of impromptu tuning. Mike was trapped. Two bulky men of ample means and girth eased him in between them, and he was still there when the march rhythm finished. The odds were about ten to one against his picking a partner he already knew, so he did not try to do any manoeuvring. A young lady dressed like several on either side of her in a crinoline sailed into his arms. Apart from the small black mask which hid her eyes, she was also wearing a costly heaped up wig of grey hair. It was difficult to detect the true colour of her hair. Her perfume was discreet and alluring. She had good teeth and smiled easily, making dimples in her plump cheeks. He felt that she had a pleasing personality, and he liked the way in which she responded to his slightest efforts.

'I think we have not met before, *señorita. Encantada.*'

He spoke to her in the language of bull fights. She understood him, but replied — to his surprise — in English. Not the adopted English of North America but of Great Britain. Moreover, he felt that she had been to an expensive finishing school.

'I am pleased to meet you, *Señor* Bull Fighter, for the first time, but I am not really conversant with the Spanish tongue. You must forgive me.

Mike laughed lightly. 'The masks are supposed to spring surprises on people, but you have surprised me already. I think you and I are probably the only two people in the building who come from the United Kingdom. What a happy coincidence that the dance should have thrown us together!'

Mike continued to move her expertly about the floor, dodging a couple here, taking advantage of a space there. Nearing the edge of the floor, he gripped her right hand a little tighter in order to swing her about. For the first time since they had come together she showed dismay.

'What is it, what have I done, miss?'

'It's my hand. You couldn't help it. It was crushed a little during a spell of horse riding. I am not really expert on horseback, you see. Your ring . . . '

As Mike released her hand, so the music changed and the short bewitching spell was over. He called a belated farewell, slipped away into the male circle and cursed himself for wearing the ring on his left hand instead of the accustomed right. The circles made one circuit of the floor. Mike accepted an overblown woman of matronly years who might have been a sister or a cousin of the hostess. She muttered in scarcely intelligible French, as though recalling the lyrics to the music.

The music changed several times more, and Mike found himself questing this way and that, trying to find out exactly where his intriguing English contact was. By the time he had located her, the dance was over and she was making a detour to avoid the attentions of a huge man with a walrus moustache.

Such was his haste to renew acquaintance that he almost fell over her at the foot of a staircase towards the rear of the room. Her mask impeded her gaze a little, but she paid immediate attention when he touched her left hand quite lightly.

'Hello again, *Señor* Toreador. The change of music cut us off rather quickly, didn't it?'

'It surely did. I wanted to apologise to you for what I did to your hand with the massive Beauclerc ring. I don't even know why I was wearing it on that hand. But it won't happen again. Here, let me take it off, anyway.'

He removed it from his finger and was about to slip it into a small pocket of his bolero. She asked to be allowed to see it, and marvelled at its impressive chunky design.

'I believe you must be a person of some consequence, sir,' she remarked quizzically, as he slipped it out of sight.

Mike shrugged. 'I'm not a Beauclerc, if that's what you think. The ring has to do with my employment. The strings started up again, making ordinary conversation more difficult. 'Up these stairs, across the gallery and down the other stairs are a number of valuable paintings and figurines. May I have the pleasure of showing some of them to you? I know several of the pieces through my work.'

The eyes behind the mask fluttered briefly as the comely young woman looked about her, no doubt seeking to trace the doings of her immediate companions, but she nodded enthusiastically and accepted gratefully.

Other, more bulky couples, ensured that they were often crushed close together. Mike almost forgot the purpose of his being there, he was so transported for a short while.

He showed her four matching miniatures, allowed her to handle two of the jade figurines, and handed over an ornate Japanese fan for her to use. The girl examined the fan, guessed at its origin, used it and ignored one or two disapproving looks from guests who did not think the objects ought to be handled.

Eventually, Mike sniffed and raised his voice. 'I believe I have the right to show these to my friends. After all, I ordered them to be brought here, and they are still in my care!'

His partner turned away, smiling broadly. A slow continuous stream of strollers went by. 'Such a temptation to anyone who might be dishonest. Not just ordinary thieves, either. Pickpockets, too, I suppose.'

Mike winced at the very thought. 'I say, do you think we could exchange identities now, or is it too early?'

'I'm as intrigued as you are, sir, but ought we not to wait until unmasking time? Prolong the mystery until then?'

'We may not be together then!' Mike protested gently.

The girl at once nodded her head, very decidedly. However, before she could say more, an elderly woman's scream of horror cut through the closing music of another dance and effectively killed the spiral of conversation which habitually built up at such a time.

'My bag! My vanity bag, it's gone! Wherever can it be? I put my earrings in it! Help, somebody. Help!'

The English girl's lips rounded into an 'O' of surprise. In spite of Mike's mask, she could detect the depth of feeling he was experiencing. She swayed closer. Side by side, they regarded the lower level of the dance floor, from where the cry had come.

4

The wine waiters had just finished circulating when the stricken female's cry impinged upon the atmosphere. It left Mike Liddell with a sense of foreboding: a feeling that all was not well, and that it was likely to get worse from that moment forward.

The voice was that of a Frenchwoman of the upper classes, who spoke English as though it had been learned from text books, rather than through balanced conversations with linguists.

'Oh, *ma vie*, won't someone help me? I feel as if I am a stranger in a foreign land. Where, where is my host, *Monsieur* Dupont?'

The crowd eased their bated breath. Many eyes looked past the bulky figure in the gold sequined dress who looked as if she was attempting to lasso herself with a stole shimmering in the same colour. Eventually, Alphonse Dupont who was more at home in a boardroom than in a salon cleared his throat with a nervous cough, and hesitatingly moved towards the dance floor from his alcove. Behind him, his wife rose and seated herself twice, each time bringing up the lorgnettes to her eyes as she did so.

'Jean-Jacques, where are you?' the host asked. 'Can anyone see my aide *Monsieur* Perçot? Ah, Didier, my boy, go and fetch Jean-Jacques, tell him to come at once. Say it is an emergency. If you can't find him, ask the *agent* to step inside. What, what do they call an *agent* in this country?'

Didier hastily discarded his cello. He bent over Isabel, murmured something in her ear, and backed off the dais, heading for the front door.

Meanwhile, Mike touched his partner in a light shoulder embrace.

'I think a search will be made in a short time. Alas, my work has to do with security. I think we shall have to part. But I would like us to meet again, if possible. What do you think?'

'I feel that way, too. It is a pity this has happened, but perhaps Madame de Boulestin is making too much of the incident. Maybe she has merely mislaid her bag. I, too, have commitments. If we could make our way downstairs and part at the foot, please.'

Mike edged her through the guests who were peering over the gallery rail and slowly piloted her down the stairs. Their movement drew a lot of attention. For a minute or more, they were the only people on the move, other than the host and his son. A noise by the main front door hushed a determined murmur prompted by curiosity. Into view came Didier, followed by Henry van Dune, the town marshal and his deputy, Jake Read. Backing the three of them were other men, ordinary constables, alerted by Didier when he went looking for Perçot. The constables merely took over as guards.

'Papa, I have with me Town Marshal van Dune, the senior *agent* and his assistant, Deputy Read. *Monsieur* van Dune has a suggestion to make.'

Another short period of suspense occurred while the two male Duponts conferred in the middle of the dance floor with the two peace officers.

Alphonse, sided by his son, then attempted to stand to his full height, in spite of his stiff, scholarly stoop.

'*Messieurs mesdames*, honoured guests, we do not wish to put you all to any great trouble. We are sure you will understand our motives behind the present course of action.' A few consecutive nervous coughs, and then Alphonse resumed. 'We ask that all ladies and gentlemen come down onto this floor. We would like the gentlemen then to separate from the ladies, and to unmask when we ask you. Er, we don't want to separate families, of course. That is not our policy. Please, if you will foregather.'

By this time, the 'wronged' lady had retired to a settee, just wide of the floor. Young Didier, whose sight was better than that of his father, could see one or two shocked expressions upon faces near him, even behind the masks. He was seemingly fearful of undiplomatic incidents.

'Papa, shouldn't we begin a search for the vanity bag? And shouldn't we ask people not to leave the room?'

Alphonse waved his son into silence. Van Dune whispered: 'My constables will stop anyone leavin' sir, an' we'll see about the search in a minute, eh?'

The families tended to move towards the area of the room where the Duponts had been seated in their alcove. Deputy Read, the former seafarer, signalled with his arms, indicating that the ladies should occupy the space behind the dais and to the left, while the gentlemen should use the dance floor, in depth, and the space to the right.

Ever since his desirable partner had slipped away, Mike had been on the alert. He had managed to move across the dais from one side to the other without attracting the attention of the peace officers. he exchanged a few notions with Isabel in Spanish while his eyes were busy. The girl seemed to have an open mind on the subject of Junoesque Madame Boulestin and her disappearing vanity bag. She could have mislaid it, or even have hidden it in order to get herself some cheap publicity. Mike thought that if Isabel was naive in matters of love, she was shrewd in dealings with older females.

Didier had been aware of the private conversation between the toreador and his delectable violinist and he was jealous. Particularly because he was not fluent in the Iberian tongue. For a short time, he held his impatience in check. This was exactly at the time when Mike made a discovery.

On the front wings of the dais, someone had placed a pair of tall china plant pots with eastern pictures on them, similar to willow pattern designs. Amid the foliage spilling out of the pot on the ladies' side of the dais, a thin gold chain sparkled, as yet unnoticed by the searchers. Mike figured it to be the holding chain of the missing vanity bag. Someone had stuffed it hurriedly into the pot while crossing the floor and the dais.

Alphonse Dupont raised his shaky voice in the centre of the floor.

'Ladies and gentlemen, if you will now remove the masks from your faces . . . and please stay still long enough for us to acquaint ourselves with your features. Thank you.'

Didier was closer and less respectful.

'You, *monsieur*, in the bull fighting outfit. If you please. Retire to the gentlemen's side of the stage.'

'I have a very good reason for staying closer, *Monsieur* Dupont. It has to do with security.'

Mike half turned away, as if he was about to resume his conversation with Isabel, but the girl had turned also and was seeing to the safety of her violin. Young Dupont pressed his advantage.

'For goodness' sake, *monsieur*, do

you think the Duponts would organise a reception such as this without adequate security? Be off with you. Join the other gentlemen, at once.'

Mike changed to speaking in French to add emphasis to his words.

'I do, *monsieur*, and I have seen and heard enough to know that you are a fool. If you are to survive in this part of the world, you will need to find out who your friends are, quite quickly.'

Clearly, the young man was shaken, but Mike stepped away in the desired direction. He moved easily, and took the opportunity to light up a small cigar. Eventually, he took up a position some five yards wide of the dais on the side used by the men. Didier kept glancing back at him, but Marshal van Dune and his father drew him into the business of looking over the faces of the men. Mike found himself being steered by the tide. Several men were delaying their own appraisal and it was in them that his own interest lay. More and more men were scrutinised. Over on the far side of the room, Madame Dupont stopped flaunting her dominating figure for the benefit of the families assembled there, and turned her attention to the small groups of ladies.

Presently, the few suspect guests were being herded towards the middle of the dance floor. The town marshal and his deputy did most of the herding, while Didier and his father did the checking and maintained a stiff overbearing manner. Mike, who was interested in possible gatecrashers, allowed himself to be herded with the others. Clearly, Didier was keen to have him removed by the peace officers. Madame Dupont showed a certain shrewdness when she stepped nearer to the dais and cleared her throat.

'May I suggest.' The murmurings ceased. 'May I suggest that some of our gentlemen, volunteers, preferably, make a search of some of the obvious places, in case the missing item has simply been overlooked, or dropped. Thank you. If you are in doubt, *messieurs*, ask my husband!'

She left a vacuum after her interference, and nearly a minute went by before the two male Duponts reacted. Mike decided that no one was going to the plant pot to get the bag, so he avoided the outstretched arm of Didier, ran over to the pot, withdrew the object and held it up. On the way back to the centre of the floor, he shook off the soil and dusted it a little under his arm.

The younger Dupont held out his hand for it, but Mike eluded him again and presented it to his father.

'May I look inside?' he asked politely, as spontaneous applause broke out from the guests. Marshal van Dune attempted to shove Mike aside, but the young Texan had the weight to withstand him, and he succeeded in opening the bag and confirming that the two earrings were inside it. 'There, Monsieur Dupont, why not return the bag to Madame Boulestin and let the festivities continue?'

The ex-banker nodded, smiled briefly and turned away. Didier contrived to get the bag away from his father and wave it in the air as he carried out the errand. In the meantime, Deputy Read was gradually coaxing three men whose unmasked faces were unfamiliar to the Duponts in the direction of the front door. On the way, two of them mentioned the name of Perçot but as Perçot had absented himself the deputy paid no heed to their protests.

'And now, it is your turn, sir,' the banker began formerly.

Mike bowed. 'Michel Bonnard Liddell, at your service, *Monsieur*. Business manager and security officer to Madame la Baronne de Beauclerc. Currently here in her stead, and alerted to guard Beauclerc valuables.'

The banker was taken aback, but he managed to smile and bow, in his turn.' Ah yes, so sorry we have not been formally introduced. Perhaps you will be kind enough to show your credentials to my son, or the town marshal, here.'

With that, Alphonse Dupont backed away and went in search of his wife. The strings began to tune up again, prior to playing another dance tune, and Mike was left with Didier and the marshal.

He was grinning as he plunged his hand into the bolero pocket where he had secreted the ring. Even when his hand came out, holding nothing more than a long narrow pink piece of scented ribbon his facial expression was a warm one.

'Alas, gentlemen, my Beauclerc ring has been removed from my pocket. But do not think of robbery. A lady whose company I found pleasing has exchanged it for a ribbon, no doubt to ensure that we shall come together again later. I'm sure this explanation is enough to a Gallic person like yourself, M. Dupont.'

But Didier's ego began to inflate

again. He sensed that Liddell was losing the initiative. Putting a false smile on his face, and gestured with his hands.

'All right, we understand an affair of the heart. What about your invitation card? That will do.'

The orchestra swung into action, couples surged onto the floor, and the three men had perforce to get out of the way. Mike indicated that he would have to go back to the cloakroom. He led the way. The corridors were quiet, but the changing room itself was almost over-crowded. Three men, who had but recently been decked out in costumes to make them like Robin Hood, Friar Tuck and King Henry VIII of England, were slowly clambering into their street attire.

Mike moved through them amiably enough. He nudged aside the deputy, who had the gun belts and guns of all three retiring 'guests' over his arms, and reached towards the hook where his shirt and pants were hanging. He had pockets on the shirt, both piped with a coloured fringe. His brow furrowed as he debated briefly in his thoughts what the odds were of being disappointed once again. It became clear that the three men, all slightly the worse for wine, and all arguing that they had acquired tickets from Perçot, were being taken down to the local lock-up in the peace office.

The flaps of the two pockets on the shirt were both undone. There was nothing inside either, except for a small cigar which had been broken in two.

Mike swore rather bitterly, facing the wall. 'Madame la Baronne's personal invitation has been removed from my pocket. How anyone could do that, when they are already indoors, I fail to understand. I can't show you my credentials, gents, but you marshal, and your depty, will recall that I showed you both a ring and card outside, in front of the house. It seems ironic to me that a security person should have his identification stolen and then be upbraided for it in the house where he is on duty!'

The six men were all slightly bowled over by the sudden intensity of Mike's outburst.

Presently, a bulky balding fellow in his late thirties spoke up.

'Hey, Paddy, do you think this bloke is accusin' us of pickin' his pocket? Me, I don't like accusations, either in parties or anywhere else!'

The speaker had a Scottish accent. The man to whom his remarks were addressed moved around with a deceptive crouching stoop. In fact he would have made a better 'Hunchback of Notre Dame' than the 'Friar Tuck' of English legend.

'Don't bother your head, Jack. This here is a reasonable sort of fellow. If he comes along with us to the peace office, we can play a four at cards, and while we're away things will start disappearing, and then they'll know we're innocent. Right?'

The Irishman winked at Mike, who could not resist the inclination to wink back again.

Didier was saying: 'I believe we're fully justified in asking this er, Bonnard person, to go along to the peace office with your deputy, Marshal van Dune. How do you see the situation?'

Van Dune saw this as an opportunity to acquire a bit of much-wanted prestige. 'Exactly my own thoughts, Mr Dupont. You go back to the dance. I'll join you when we've seen these gents on their way.'

Mike remarked: 'You do know you have at least two ladies of impeccable breeding in there who could vouch for me anywhere, don't you?'

In fact, he was exaggerating a little, but he felt that he could count upon his as-yet unnamed lady friend, as well as Isabel.

Deputy Read urged his three charges out of the room. Didier intimated by eye glances that the marshal should send Liddell after them. Mike, who could quite easily have given them a whole lot of trouble, elected to go along with the other three on the offchance that they had already removed items of great value, or were in touch with others who would do so.

'I'll change when we get to the peace office,' the Texan decided. 'In the meantime, Didier, you'd better pray you haven't got any expert jewel thieves loose in that house. If you have, you'll have a devil of a job with only a rooky marshal and a few green constables. Buenas noches.'

So saying, Mike picked up his outdoor clothes and left his gun belt for van Dune to collect. As the four evicted men, closely watched by the deputy and two constables, went off up the street, the lilting sound of dance music pursued them.

Mike trudged through the dirt with mixed feelings. He knew one thing, he was more concerned about the mystery girl with the English accent than he was about Madame's valuables and the loss of face occasioned by the Duponts' attitude seemed less hurtful when he thought of her.

5

On the way to the peace office, several fellows lolling about on the sidewalks jeered at the quartet with the official escort. The Scot and the Irishman, however, paid little heed, having imbibed quite a quantity of liquor before they were evicted. Ben Trine, who had passed himself off as Robin Hood, whistled all the way and showed quite a bit of interest in Mike, not knowing what sort of intruder he had turned out to be.

Soon they were in the main part of the office, and the eyes of Trine were more active than those of his companions. Mike watched him. He was apparently checking the walls for signs of reward notices, and also attempting to examine the possibilities connected with their temporary incarceration. There was a temporary cell against the rear wall of the office, but really there was not enough room for four men who had been living it up until a short while ago.

Jack Fender and Wally Hexham were propping each other up in the friendliest fashion by the time Deputy Read had unlocked the door to the cell block jutting out down a corridor. Trine then showed how wide awake he was.

'If it's all the same to you, deputy, me an' my buddy, here, we'll take the far cell at the end of the line. How will that be? We're wide awake, you see, an' the night is young, so we thought we'd play a few hands at cards. You yourself will be goin' back to the big house, I take it? On account of there bein' free drinks for the helpers at the end of the evenin' as likely as not.'

Read was a man of few words. From time to time, he chuckled as if chuckling was a way of answering anyone speaking to him. He housed Trine and Liddell in the end cell and soon locked them in. Mike at once began to divest himself of the toreador outfit, and replaced his ordinary walking out gear. The night was warm, but not warm enough to sleep in a cell with an open grille and bars for a wall.

Fender and Hexham, chuckling and fumbling, were put into the next cell where they sprawled about, attempting to tell one another jokes and forgetting the details before the end.

Trine stood holding onto the bars as Read backed away. He reminded the deputy that he was expecting the loan of a pack of cards before they were left on their own.

This time, Read actually talked to them. 'All right, I'll get you the cards, friend. A word of advice, too. If you are hoping to get out through that door with the grille in it, don't bother. It's been rusted up for years. Rest easy, why don't you? The constable will bring you the cards. As for me, I'll be away to drink some of that rum punch. I developed a liking for the devil's liquor when I made me livin' in deep waters. *Adios*, friends.'

The deputy and the constable who had accompanied him down the corridor withrew into the office. Trine then hastily examined the door Read had mentioned. It was made of metal and a good proportion of the outer edges were indeed well rusted. Trine and Mike backed away from the grille as the hollow eyed constable came back through the door which gave access to the corridor.

They received the cards: also two blankets apiece. The Scotsman and the Irishman began to sing, but it was clear that they would fall asleep before they had rendered many verses.

Mike gave his partner a small cigar and lighted one for himself.

Trine sucked on his and strolled up and down in his stockinged feet. From time to time, he chuckled and scratched himself above the belt level. The lamp in the corridor flickered as if the paraffin was getting low, but after a while it recovered. The area brightened as the singers, now silent, slumped into their blanket bedrolls.

'Could I ask you a question, amigo?' Trine whispered.

'The name is Mike. Mike Liddell. What is your question, Ben?'

'You're in a cell now, but hell, that could happen to anyone. Can I ask you, do you have your name on a reward notice anywhere?'

'Not that I know of, Ben. But there might be a reward out some place to have me removed altogether. In my security work, I tend to rub some hombres up the wrong way. Now, why don't we get down to a few hands of cards, while those who have too much goin' for them make out they're enjoyin' themselves?'

Trine brightened up quite suddenly. He gave out with a braying laugh which sounded quite unusual when heard the first time.

'Pontoon, then, at four bits a go. What do you say, Michael?'

'I'm all in favour, so long as it doesn't

take all night. Your two mates snorin'
seem to be gettin' through to me. Here
goes.'

The twenty-one game kept them
quiet for upwards of a half hour. Trine
won the first two goes. Mike then won
one, and Trine collected another two.
After that, Mike picked up three times
on the run and subsequently the
honours were more or less even. A
slight scraping noise at first failed to
draw their attention, but when it was
repeated first one and then the other
gave it a small amount of attention.

'What in tarnation is that, Mike?
Surely they don't have rats in a clean
jail like this?'

'I'm baffled, Ben,' Mike admitted.
'It's comin' from some place at floor
level, an' yet it hasn't anything to do
with the sleepers. More in the region of
our rusted door, but surely it couldn't
be that. Could it?'

Both men needed an extra card to
settle the current game. The rustling
noise, therefore, was ignored for a

minute or two. It was while Mike was shuffling the cards that his partner's mouth dropped open. Trine lost the butt of his cigar which had long since gone out. He snapped his fingers and pointed.

Mike's sensitive fingers closed on the paste boards. 'I don't believe it. If you're stringin' me along, Ben, you're doin' a good job. Tell me, do you have a partner on the outside who is alerted to get you out of here?'

The braying laugh again. 'My luck comes an' goes. Not that I know of anyone waitin' for me outside. These two here sleepin', Jack Fender an' Wally Hexham are my only buddies in this area. Neither of them are suited to workin' the houses of the rich, especially when there's liquor about. But, well, they ain't expectin' anybody otherwise why would they be asleep when a key starts to work its way under the door from the outside?'

Mike shrugged and put aside the cards. By this time, both of them were equally fascinated by the end of a substantial rusty key which had been recently oiled. Perhaps another inch of it came under the door and then it remained still.

'Is it stuck, do you think?' Mike whispered.

'How would it be if we called that ghoul of a constable an' told him some dishonest jasper is tryin' to break into our cell?'

'You can't be serious, Ben!' Mike protested.

Ben exercised his braying laugh, once again. This time it was louder, but in spite of its unusual timbre it did not disturb the two sleepers in the next cell. Nor did it invoke any sort of sound from out of doors.

Eventually, Trine tiptoed over to the door, knelt down and took a grip of the key. Before tugging on it, he tilted his head back and looked up at Mike who was on tiptoe above him, peering through the grille and into the gloom beyond.

'Anything?'

'Nothing. Let's give it a go.'

Trine worked the key indoors, becoming breathless with the exertion. At the same time, Mike worked his way round the surface of the door, checking whether it was actually rusted to the frame.

'Sure does seem strange, havin' a metal door in a spot like this. An' there's another unusual angle to it, as well. Unless I'm mistaken, it opens outwards. Does that seem strange to you, Ben?'

'Sure, it's strange, amigo, but who cares, if it provides an early exit out of a spot like this? After all, if we stayed to breakfast that self-important town marshal might drum up some other charge against us apart from gatecrashing. So here goes.'

He inserted the key in the lock, whistled an owl hoot through the grille and waited in vain for a similar reply. 'If we get out, will you come with us, Mike?'

Mike nodded. 'My business is back there, in the big house. Not here in the hoosegow. So, how are you doin'?'

Trine worked hard to the turn the key. It fitted all right, but getting it to turn was another matter. He wrestled with it, lost his breath and hastily brushed perspiration from his brow and moustache with an adroit back and forth movement. Mike relieved him. He put pressure on the key with both hands, took a deep breath and writhed with the effort. The key gave way so suddenly that at first the young Texan thought the vital piece of metal had snapped. Not so. It had turned through a half circle. He exchanged glances with his partner, then carefully turned it the other half.

'No one out there willin' to show himself,' Mike remarked breathlessly. 'If the galoot has already moved off, we can throw a lot of weight against the door and still get out. Comprende?'

'Comprende.' Ben rolled up his sleeves, signalled for Mike to keep out of the way, and threw his right shoulder against the metal, just below the grille. The door shuddered, and shook, but did not give altogether. Trine retired, holding his aching shoulder and willingly agreed to Mike taking over. Mike tried once to no avail, then tried again with one hand on the door knob, making sure it was turned to the maximum. This time the whole door gave way and he had to hold himself back, otherwise he would have been precipitated into the open air.

Trine laughed with relief and excitement. His glance went back up the corridor. For the first time he was wondering if the constable was still awake and alert in the main office. Mike followed his questing eyes. They both listened hard and waited, but no sort of reaction came from the office. Either it was empty, or the constable was asleep. It was beyond the bounds of probability that he was extremely deaf.

'He'll be doin' the rounds, I guess. Not to worry. However, if we're goin' to avail ourselves of this unexpected opportunity, we ought to be makin' a move real soon. Life sure as hell is unpredictable in these parts. I think you ought to have the first opportunity, Ben. Too bad we don't have a gun or two. Seein' as how it's really dark out there now. But perhaps we're lookin' on the black side of things.'

Trine produced a coin, tossed it up. Mike called and called wrong.

'Okay, I'll go first,' Ben conceded. 'Give me a minute. If nothing has happened by then, wake the others and follow me yourself. Does that sound reasonable?'

Mike was thinking quickly. He had permitted himself to be incarcerated in order to find out information from these three. And here he was, aiding and abetting them to make their escape. However, they did not appear to have done any serious crimes at the Dupont house, so what did it matter? Gate-crashing in itself was only a modest form of illegal entry. Not worth depriving a man of his liberty for. He shrugged to himself.

'Sure, Ben. If anythin' looks suspicious, though, don't be afraid to come back in. I'm sure you follow my line of reasonin'.'

Troubleshooter and villain shook hands with each other. Ben struggled into his boots. Mike took another long probing look through the grille, but failed to detect any sort of movement. He indicated as much. Mike finally took charge of the door knob. He turned it, Ben ghosted through the gap and he closed it again. Trine obviously moved away from the back of the building quite quickly, but he went silently and Mike found himself counting off the seconds up to sixty. Nothing had occurred by the end of the count.

He was about to pull on his own boots when a single gunshot, out at the back, boomed across the open space and the shock made him straighten up and stiffen. His eye glance was fixed on the grille, wondering if any other shot was to follow. He felt sure that it had been a hand gun, but who had fired it? Ben did not have one, so it must have been the person who had provided the key. Always supposing that the shot and the key incident were linked.

Hexham and Fender had both stirred in their sleep due to the gunfire, but neither of them had roused. Mike, as a result, felt quite isolated: quite alone. He had one or two initiatives, but not much that he could do with guaranteed safety. In the back of his mind, he held the conviction that the bullet had been fired at Ben Trine. Already, he was assuming that Ben was out of action: either wounded or dead.

He looked down at his boots, thought about throwing one at the door to the office. If he did, and there was no response, he would be left with one boot. What could he do otherwise? The dark opening which was the barred grille appeared to grow bigger. He could go over there and take another look out. In doing so, he would be challenging the unknown. If there was a killer out there, what could be easier than firing a bullet at a head outlined behind a grille in lamplight?

The creased well-worn boots of Jack Fender, standing side by side near the common wall of bars, seemed to be the answer. Fender would not be in a fit condition to do anything in a hurry, in any case, if another incident occurred . . .

It was easy enough to acquire the two boots. A slight odour came from within, an odour which no doubt would have given offence at the Dupont reception if Fender had not been wearing a pair of sandals.

Having transferred the boots to his own cell, Mike then made one or two practice swings with one of them. As he did so, he supposed that no other prisoners had behaved in exactly this sort of fashion since the peace office had been built. He swung the boot in a clockwise direction. The first time something made him retain his hold.

The second time, he put much more effort behind his swing. Consequently, the boot flew higher than he had intended. It struck the ceiling of the passageway, ricocheted onwards, and finally hit the corridor door with its heel, producing a substantial noise.

Bluey Dunstable, the temporary constable, who had only been back in the office following a walk-around for two minutes, jerked forward in the marshal's swivel chair with an almighty shock. He had been just about to doze off to sleep. His shotgun lay across the desk top, and his gun belt and holster were draped across his knees.

Bluey, a forty year old ex-sailor who had jumped ship on the west coast of USA and stayed for good, wondered if his authority was going to be challenged. First, something which sounded like a gun shot. Then this bang against the door to the cell block. What next?

A further bang from the corridor as he was standing with his bowed legs apart, buckling on his belt. He blinked his eroded eyes several times, and stroked his drooping moustache. If one of the prisoners was loose, surely trouble would reach him at the communicating door. But nothing further happened.

He moved towards it, quickly and quietly, and listened. Muted snoring was all he heard. He could ignore the sounds which had occurred, but in doing so he could put himself at peril. So, steeling himself for the worst, he unlocked the door, slowly opened it and then sprang through it. No one was waiting to jump him. Moreover, down the corridor he could see the recumbent sleeping forms in the nearer of the two occupied cells.

'Constable, come down here, will you? You may have lost a prisoner!'

The voice was the authoritative one of the fair Texan who claimed to have a connection with the other French residence in Sundown City.

'Why do you hesitate?' the same

speaker queried. 'You've got weapons, haven't you?'

'Why you can't sleep off that wine an' leave men who have work to do in peace, I really can't say,' Bluey retorted. 'Now, what's this about losin' a prisoner?'

He moved slowly along the corridor, his shotgun at the ready, and his questing eyes searching every bit of shadow for the fourth man. Eventually, he came to a halt about a yard away from Liddell, who said: 'I threw the boots at the door. Seemed to be the best way of attracting your attention. My partner, he went out, that way.'

Dunstable gave a dry throaty laugh. 'Oh, no, he didn't. That door hasn't been opened since President Lincoln's day, so help me.'

Rather than argue, Mike stepped to the door, turned the key a couple of times, opened the door a few inches and then closed it again. Dunstable was impressed.

'He could have been shot. Someone

fired a gun back there shortly after he went out. He's made no contact since. We need someone with a weapon to investigate.'

Dunstable shifted his weight from one bowed leg to the other. He was shaken by this development, but uppermost in his mind was the realisation that he had lost a prisoner.

'You knew he was goin', troubleshooter. Now, you step through the door an' see what's happened to him,' Dunstable advised.

Mike shrugged and looked away. Almost as an afterthought, he turned back again. 'I'll do it if you'll hand me a gun. A six-shooter will do. Otherwise, you'll have to come through an' investigate for yourself!'

Dunstable backed further away from the bars, shaking his head.

'Whoever heard of a constable handin' a prisoner a loaded gun? I wasn't born yesterday, friend. I'm forty years of age. Aim to go on tottin' up my score, too. So think again, amigo.'

This time, Mike really did turn his back upon the constable. He moved over to the sleeping bunk, worked his way into the blankets and went through the motions of composing himself for sleep.

'You're the boss, constable. Do it your way. Mind you, the marshal won't be too pleased when he gets back here.'

Mike settled himself back and closed his eyes. Dunstable, meanwhile, deliberated rather ponderously. Eventually, he decided that he would have to investigate further by going through the cell. He unlocked the door, stepped inside and turned his back on the recumbent prisoner, which was his undoing.

Mike rose quietly to his feet, waited for the constable to turn round and hit him with a measured blow to the chin. Dunstable's teeth grated together, he gasped, opened his mouth wide and then lost his senses. There was no necessity for a further blow. Instead, Mike removed the shotgun from the other's grasp and allowed him to slide to the floor.

The initiative was now in young Liddell's hands. He took a few deep breaths and looked around him. Less than a minute elapsed before Dunstable was between the blankets and Mike was into his boots. And still the neighbours, Fender and Hexham slept on. Should they be freed?

Mike ran for the boots which he had thrown. He recovered them, hurled them into the sleepers' cell and also hurled the bunch of keys in after them.

'Wake up, you two, it's time to go! You hear me? Rouse yourselves, Trine has gone already, and there'll be trouble for you when the marshal gets back! Hurry it up!'

He then dashed to the office, collected his personal gear and went back to the cells, where he explained how Trine had gone through the rusty door. He added a warning that he might have been shot by an unknown assailant, and wished them well. Both men were red-eyed but they had sufficient control to make a proper effort.

Avoiding the back way, Mike went through the office and cautiously stepped out onto the sidewalk. There was noise abroad. Some of it was impromptu merrymaking, but there was more to it than that. Ominous sounds suggested there was some sort of search afoot. Instinctively, the fugitive avoided the bright lights.

6

The atmosphere of tension combined with the efforts he had put into getting out of the cell boosted Mike's spirits, so that as he dodged from one alleyway to another, using the shadows, he felt elated and wide awake in spite of the hour being a little after midnight.

He felt that at the witching hour a man ought to be able to pursue his own pursuits and, as his brief sojourn with the English girl was still vivid in his mind, he brushed aside troubling thoughts about the fate of Ben Trine and thought about furthering his acquaintance with the lady.

A fellow who had managed to cadge a few drinks at the big house for doing odd jobs informed him that the orchestra had just ceased to function and that people who were not sleeping in the house had started to make their way to their lodgings.

While he was still in the house earlier, he had heard that there were many more guests than there were bedrooms. Another notion made him think that his lady friend would be one of those to seek lodgings elsewhere. But where? He had to be careful who he approached for information, especially as there seemed to be some sort of hunt going on for a malefactor. Besides, the town marshal and several of his peace-keeping entourage knew him by sight. And that could only mean trouble, if they set eyes on him.

He bribed a man settling down to sleep in the open with one of his small cigars. Armed with the location of two of the most likely rooming houses for well-to-do folks from out of town, he dashed to find his acquaintance before they all put out the lamps for the night.

At the first place, he almost stumbled over a man reclining on the gallery in a rocking chair. The fellow drew up his slippered feet, full of hostility. He listened with dwindling patience to Mike's questions, and then explained that he was the permanent lodger and that the lady of the house only took in male guests.

A black and a white girl simpering and giggling on the first floor balcony of the second location gave Mike the notion that it was not an ordinary rooming house at all. When a small patrol headed by constables began to work their way through the area, he lost confidence in his immediate quest and used his wits and his knowledge of the town to avoid busy thoroughfares and human entanglements. So far, he was assuming that no one had been back to the peace office and found out the fate of Constable Dunstable.

There was the matter of Ben Trine's fate, too. Sooner or later, someone or another was bound to find out about the gun shot at the back of the peace office. As Mike reflected, he knew in his own mind that he had already written off his former cell mate as dead.

Something about the whole situation made him shudder. He had never felt quite so insecure since he first came into the county and began his relationship with the Beauclerc menage.

He had a lot to learn about the night's happenings and some of it was bound to be unpleasant. Nearing the Dupont house, he dumped his dressing up clothes over a short hedge, checked that his .45 Colt was in full working order and started to think out what his approach was going to be this time.

A Mexican constable was walking up and down in a disconsolate fashion, wearily acting the part of a guard while others took on more serious duties indoors.

'Buenas tardes, señor,' Mike began, in his best Spanish. 'I am Michael Liddell, in charge of security at the Chateau Beauclerc in Sundown. I went up to the peace office, on account of a little misunderstanding, but it is all cleared up now. Perhaps you will be kind enough to show me indoors? I need to take a look at some expensive ornaments on loan to the house from my mistress.'

'*Momento, señor*, the town marshal, he is very strict, an' since valuable objects have been moved, it has become worse.'

The constable stepped up the shallow wooden stairs at the front and entered the foyer. Moving with commendable quietness, Mike went after him. There was a sudden altercation between the Mexican and the town marshal, who was actually on his way to the outer door to throw away a cigar butt. The sight of Mike, who should have been in a cell, took van Dune's angry breath away. While the marshal was gasping, Mike made a little headway, laying on a beatific smile before he began his explanation.

'Here we are again, marshal. I've recovered from the unfortunate incident which ended in Madame la Baronne de Beauclerc's accredited agent being taken along to the peace office on a trumped up excuse. On this occasion, I am hesitating whether to make a full report about your conduct to la Baronne and her influential friends at county level. But I'm not pleased, not pleased at all to be so treated.'

Van Dune did not know whether to bluster or become obsequious. 'Tell me one thing, Liddell — all right, Mr Liddell. How did you manage to quit the cell without my authority?'

Mike glared at him. 'Fortunately for you, Constable Dunstable decided to unlock my door, no doubt thinking an injustice had been perpetrated. I fancy he's worked in this county a whole lot longer than you have, marshal. Now, be good enough to escort me further indoors. I've heard rumours of valuables goin' missing an' I want to check if any of them belong to la Baronne.'

Van Dune was still not convinced that he ought to accede to Liddell's wishes, but Mike urged him forward, pushed him in the back, in fact, and the two of them arrived in the deserted expanse which had so recently been a ballroom. Upright chairs were loosely stacked. The air reeked of stale tobacco and cigar smoke, and the cloying smell of many perfumes.

'All right, marshal, I believe I can find my way about now,' Mike murmured confidentially.

From half way up the staircase to the gallery, Didier Dupont called out in a semi-hysterical tone. '*Ma vie*, how on earth did *that* fellow get back in here? I thought we'd seen the last of him for tonight! Really, this is too much, Liddell. I'll have to ask you to clear out. Good grief, man, we've lost things. We're upset. This is not the time for you to come prowling around asking questions. It's too late, or too early, and I've got a headache. Marshal, show him out. You know what to do.'

Mike ignored the marshal, and walked forward, slowly ascending the steps. Half way up, the highly strung young Dupont extended an arm and pointed with a finger which shook.

'Look here, my father won't have you in the house. I *insist* you go!'

Mike kept walking until Didier had to withdraw his arm. Their faces were only a foot apart when Mike gave his answer. 'Your father was not too proud to borrow from others to make this barn of a house look pretty. As for me, I refuse to leave while madame's property is here, at risk.'

Eventually, Didier backed down. 'Oh, very well, but I won't have our house guests disturbed tonight. Do you understand? You must go to a bedroom in the far wing, and stay there! Come, I'll show you to your room myself!'

Mike courteously bowed and gave ground. The weary marshal hurried away on some pretext or other. Powder and footmarks had marked the carpets in places. Here and there, a muffled giggle came from an imposing door to a bedroom suite. Mike wondered where Isabel was located, but he did not ask. They found a room, and Mike lighted the hanging lamp. Didier checked that the bed had been made up and the curtains drawn.

After drawing his six-gun, giving it a roll by the trigger guard and restoring it to the holster, Mike removed his hat and skimmed it onto the bed.

'Feel free to call me, if you have any further emergencies, *monsieur*,' he murmured, oozing with mock politeness.

Didier sighed temperamentally, and withdrew.

★　★　★

Mike was still overcharged with energy in spite of the hour. He paced up and down for a good ten minutes, and then decided that he had to find his female acquaintance, or Isabel: or get some vital information about properties and the English girl's whereabouts.

He crossed to the substantial door without having any clear plan in mind. It would not open. Didier had put one over on him. The Frenchman had locked the door on the outside. Mike grudgingly grinned. Didier certainly did not lack spirit, even if some of the previous day and that night were a little too much for him.

Mind pictures floated through the frustrated trouble-shooter's mind. He saw Deputy Read releasing Constable Dunstable from the cells, remonstrating with him about all the prisoners being loose. And, in a further scene, a great deal more anger being generated when someone or another tested the rusty getaway door, and found the dead body of one of their prisoners just beyond it. Soon, the word would get back to *this* house, to Marshal van Dune, and the marshal — although physically weary and not too adept at his job — knew the whereabouts of the Liddell character. And Liddell was one scoundrel who was not going any place until he had faced up to the father and mother of a weighty explanation. If Dunstable happened to embellish his version of peace office events, or tell a few lies, Mike could visualise himself being locked up for a long time. Also, he would ultimately embarrass Madeleine, la Baronne, and cause her to lose face with friends and acquaintances from far and wide.

A handful of hair grips, held together with a twist of wire, slowly came under the door as he was mopping fresh perspiration from his face and neck and actually looking towards the stout timbers of the door. He could have blasted his way out with a bullet or two, but that would have been unthinkable. Now, someone was presenting him with the wherewithal to get out in a less noisy fashion.

There was a pencilled note with the hair grips. It said: *Good luck with the social side of your work. Room 37, East side*.

He had seen the handwriting before. It amused and interested him. In fact, he had been very fond of Isabel before she began a passionate affair with a character who had turned out to be a renegade. But he would have preferred the note to be a *billet doux* from his mysterious new dancing partner. He went down on one knee and peered through the key hole. The key itself had been removed. Before making a tool of sorts out of the hair grips, he crossed to the window. The descent to the ground, using a rope made out of sheets, would not have been too difficult. The only difficulty would be arriving out of doors without the essential information he wanted.

Back to the door and the key hole. Picking locks was not a skill which he knew about, really, but faced with the need to go through a door an attempt had to be made. He straightened out one grip, poked it in the slot, extracted it again and put new bends in it. Scratching around, he made progress, but the grip itself was too frail for the old lock. He had to make another probe, twisting two grips together to make them thicker and stronger. At the second attempt with the new tool, the lock clicked open.

He stood up with all the dignity of a bull-fighter, briefly recollecting the fancy dress he had worn only a few hours ago. The door opened as he turned the knob. Now, to find Room 37. One thing he had noticed as Didier escorted him. The numbering of the doors. He had to retrace his steps to the main part of the floor and then go along to the other wing.

Fortunately, he had his bearings, and no one showed up to ask awkward questions on the way. Soon, he was in the secluded passage with rooms 36 to 38 in it. He tried the door very gently, found it locked, and cautiously applied his knuckles to a panel. Inside, he heard sounds: nothing very noisy, but sufficient to make him believe that the occupant had heard the knock. However, no one approached the door to let him in, and that baffled him a little. Someone in 36 was snoring powerfully. Hearing the noise he refrained from knocking louder. After repeating his first knock, he counted up to thirty and then knelt by the lock.

Smiling to himself, he applied his locking picking tool once again, and this time he managed to open the door in less time. He stepped inside and closed the main door. Ahead of him was another, less stout door leading into the bedroom proper. A door leading to a private bathroom was on his right. Making noise deliberately, using his knuckles on the bedroom door, he opened it and stepped inside, clearing his throat and looking about him. Against the far wall was a four-poster bed with pink drapes. A small smooth mound showed where the occupant was curled up in it. A familiar giggle came from near the bolster. Isabel. This was one of her mischievous little tricks.

Mike cleared his throat and began to mumble, aping the manner of Alphonse Dupont, who was not very fluent in the English language.

'La, la, what is this? What 'as been 'appening 'ere?'

Two things happened then at the same time. Isabel threw back the bed coverings, and a furtive stranger chose that moment to escape from the private bathroom, making his way into the passage and moving with haste.

Mike was convulsed with laughter. He seated himself on the foot of the bed and beamed at the plump Spanish girl who had made possible his escape with her hair grips. She was wearing a pink nightdress, in keeping with the bed drapes. Her honey blonde hair hung about her like spun silk. Behind her captivating smile, her clear grey eyes had a calculating look in them.

'So, troubleshooter, you came to me when you could have been down the stairs and away. That is good!'

Mike discarded his hat. He crossed to a sumptuous wash hand stand and studied his reflection in the mirror behind it. Golden stubble was building up on his pointed chin. His sideburns needed trimming, too. His blue eyes were bright, but developing a slightly glassy look due to lack of sleep.

'I thank you for giving some of your thoughts to me, Isabelita, but I am disturbed to note that I am not your first visitor tonight.'

The girl giggled. 'The Dupont son and heir is a very tentative slow-moving lover. He is more suited to bank boardrooms than bedrooms. Besides, you are tired. Come on over here. Let us not waste time with scruples, Michael. Come and tell me what has been happening to you. What did you do when that deputy with the brass buttons marched you away?'

Mike nodded to her reflection, in the mirror.

'All right, we'll talk. But not in bed. I would fall asleep. And, as you pointed out earlier, I *am* on duty.'

He poured water into the basin from a tall jug with a matching pattern on it. In a drawer of the stand, he found a collection of three open razors, in leather sheaths. Selecting one, he groped around for soap and a brush. Perceiving what he intended to do, Isabel slowly stood up in the bed, raising her arms.

'I could shriek and bring lots of men rushing to my bedroom to protect me. That is, if you insist upon neglecting me!'

Mike wetted his face, and rubbed soap on it. At the same time, he ogled the bewitching girl's reflection. 'Charming, I'm sure. A sight for tired eyes. Now, you were asking. Well, they put me in a cell with a fellow named Ben Trine. We played cards. Then, some mysterious fellow out at the back of the peace office slipped a key under the door. Trine got out first, and there was a gun shot. Don't know what happened to him. Wouldn't surprise me if he was killed. Me, I got out the other way. Through the office. Called the constable and thumped him. Others may come looking for me at any time. Even if they found me in this house, I'd still have to answer a lot of questions, if Trine is dead.'

Mike paused for breath. He began to shave himself with long sweeping steady strokes. Isabel had finished teasing him. She had sunk down into a kneeling position. The tip of her tongue was exploring her lips, just showing.

'Rumours suggest that other items have been stolen from this house. Do you know if any of them belonged to Madeleine? That is one of the things I need to know without delay.'

'All right, all right. I know you always put work before the more desirable side of life. As it happens, I can help you. We had to talk about something while Didier attempted to get his emotions under control. For certain, there are two Dutch miniatures missing. Probably Beauclerc paintings. Head and shoulders only. A Dutchman and his wife. And a miniature silver salver with a symbolic madonna and child upraised on it. Now, what else do you need to know?'

Isabel turned over and reached out to a shelf beyond the bed head. When she was back in the other pose, she was tilting a wine glass of champagne to her lips. Mike finished off the razor work on his throat and began to rinse the soap off himself. He felt slightly embarrassed as he changed his line of questioning.

'I danced with a young lady who had an English accent. I need to trace her. Pronto, eh? You may know her name, or where she has been accommodated.'

Isabel sighed.' So that is why you are not interested in me. An English girl. You like the French. You pretend to like the Spaniards, but all the time you want the English!'

Mike finished towelling himself and moved over to the bed. He took the glass from Isabel's hand and sipped from it. 'It isn't like that at all, Isabelita. She has my ring, the Beauclerc ring. Being without it is causing all manner of problems.'

He kissed her lightly, gave her back the glass and hoped she would believe his line of argument. She didn't seem as if she was convinced, and he did not blame her.

'She's not in the house. She's supposed to be the companion to a travelling Frenchwoman. Two or three companions were escorted over to another property, one with a Dutch name. A name associated with the early days of New York. If it's only the ring, I will lie for you, say anything you want me to. What do you say?'

'I hate myself for having to say it, Isabel, but anything between the two of us must come later. I must go now, before dawn comes up and catches me unprepared. *Hasta la vista*, my pretty little violinist.'

Another kiss and he slipped away from her. Anger dissolved on her face as she saw him make his rope out of sheets. Soon he was on his way down to the ground, occasionally brushing the outer wall with his knees or boots. One last wave, a blown kiss and he was weaving his way through the garden and thankful that the Duponts were not dog minded.

Isabel pulled up the sheets, untied them and draped them back in disorder over the top of her bed. She searched through her mind for tunes reminiscent of a runaway lover. She knew she was tormenting herself unnecessarily.

7

One hour before dawn, the streets of Riverside were still subject to visits from prowling constables. Bluey Dunstable's fate had upset the marshal quite a bit. Also the suggestion that one of his prisoners had been lured outside and shot. If that was not enough for a lot of temporary constables on good casual money, there was also the notion that a villain who had attended the reception was on the loose.

Mike asked questions twice. The first time he got no answer. The second time, the fellow decided to shout after a patrol which had only recently gone by. In order to close the lips of the would-be informer, he had to hit him quite hard.

Even then, he had to run from one street to another, with determined men following him. Presently, as his legs started to protest, he crawled under a sidewalk aware of all the dirt and waste matter he might encounter. And there he met a fellow sufferer, one who had done a lot more drinking than running.

Barney Ross had dented his derby hat in the early minutes of a chase. Since then, he had banged his nose and almost gone through the knees of his trousers as he worked on all fours.

'Are you lookin' for anywhere in particular, friend?'

Mike groaned. 'I'm lookin' for a biggish house with a Dutch name. A place where travelling ladies might be put up for the night. Do you know of such a place? Maybe 'van' something. Ever heard of Rip van Winkle, comrade?'

Mike felt that his drunken companion ought to be asking questions like that, but his powers of lucid thought had taken a beating, and they were unlikely to improve until he had slept.

'Don't tell me that marshal, van Dune, runs a hotel as well as everything else in this burg, friend. I wouldn't like

121

to be his guest not at any price. Tell you what I'll do, though. If you could lend me a bit of guidance, I'd take you to the house where my bed awaits me an' introduce you to my landlady. She stays up late all the time, doing knittin' till I get back. But one of these days, she's goin' to lose patience with me, an' that'll be my lot. Another fellow will become the cock lodger an' I'll be out on my ear. I won't be so happy, then. So, what do you say about the two of us hittin' the road in search of the house with the red gate?'

Mike agreed at once, hoping that it would not be far away and that there would not be any pitfalls on the way. In fact, the rooming house was scarcely fifty yards away: through an intersection and away to the left. Barney was a heavy burden, even though his legs still worked. As they meandered towards the small dog-soiled notorious red gate, one of the lower windows slowly opened at the bottom. A woman's round face, accentuated by a puckered cap, appeared there briefly. Satisfied that one of the pair approaching the house was her missing lodger, she wrapped her cloak-like housecoat around her and hurried to the front door.

The pair swayed on the threshold. As they did so, she savoured the expired breath coming from them. The stranger's was much less strong, fragrant almost, but she showed no particular pleasure in this discovery.

'I've brought my friend along. He's on the lookout, Mary. Do you have a Dutch house anywheres near?'

'Bring him upstairs, friend. I'll show you where to unload him. No, I don't have a Dutch house in this quarter. Why for does he want a *Dutch* house? Is he tryin' to impress the town marshal or somethin'?'

Hearing this rejoinder, Barney shook with laughter and became much more difficult to handle up the stairs. Mary's subdued voice reminded Mike of Molly O'Callan's Irish brogue, Molly being the housekeeper and companion to madame at the Beauclerc chateau.

Eventually, they had the door to Barney's room open. In he went, discarding the support of both of them, and plunging head first towards his bed. A heap of small coins shot out of the pockets of his waistcoat as he made contact, and within seconds he started to snore.

Mary crooked a finger, and intimated that Mike should follow her. She took him to an empty room and lit a lamp which hung on the wall of a long narrow bed.

'Friend, the streets are not healthy tonight for strangers. Take this room and sleep. I have several bodies in my quarters who are only in town temporary, but I won't have them disturbed. Not before breakfast, that's my rulin'. Van Dune's boys have called once, but I won't let them in again. So if you've done something they want you for, you can rest easy. I'll show them the shotgun if they come again. Are you stayin' then?'

'I am, Mary. I am,' Mike assured her vehemently. 'I've scarcely the strength to get into the bed. Call me if I'm sleepin' late, will you?'

She nodded gravely. He placed a silver dollar in her hand, on account of services rendered, and showed her out. His notions about good manners set her thinking, but she kept on going down the stairs, putting out lamps on the ground floor and carefully preparing to retire.

Mike's corner room was facing towards the east. Already the suspicion of greyness was distantly creeping into the sky. He had a lot on his mind, but it would have to wait. At least for a few hours.

★ ★ ★

Others, besides Barney and Mike Liddell had dodged the long arm of the law during those tricky hours when the streets were being scoured for missing prisoners and Dupont house valuables.

Wally Hexham and Jack Fender had had a busy time since Mike roused them in their warm cell and suggested that they might want to get out in a hurry. They had scoured the vacant lot at the back of the peace office for Ben Trine's body and failed to find it. All they noticed was a trace of blood, as if a wounded body had moved over the ground. Having failed to find any further trace of their partner, they retraced their steps, went out through the main office, where they collected their firearms, and entered the street with a show of boldness.

Avoiding the constables was like trying to play hide-and-seek in the dark. Somehow they had managed to stay clear of the round-up men, and when Mike had finally come away from the Dupont residence, the two former cell mates had been fortunate enough to catch sight of him. Prowling law enforcers had prevented them from getting close to him as he began to play the dodging game, but they had seen him again when he dived under the sidewalk and found the fellow Barney there.

When the two figures had staggered clear, Fender's keenness to get in touch had almost put them into the hands of two Mexican constables. They backed off, went into cover and stayed there until the swarthy patrollers had moved on.

Just when it seemed that they had lost 'sign' they found the deeply marked trail made by Barney's dragging feet, and that took them to the red gate.

Hexham limped off round the side of the house, checking up on all the detail he could find. He was fortunate enough to be standing below the right corner when a lamp blossomed into light and revealed a woman's arm and upper trunk. His beady eyes learned very little about the matronly female, but his patience was rewarded quite soon afterwards when he caught a glimpse of Mike Liddell before the lamp was extinguished again.

Fender joined him a minute later. 'So what are we waitin' for now?'

'We've found 'im. He's just settled down in that room, up there. Are you ready with the next move?'

'Now we know where he is, it's all right, ain't it? We can come back early an' grab 'im before 'e moves on. Your shifty little eyes are just about shuttin' now, Wallie. So where do we go? Want to try the same 'ouse?'

Hexham spat out a silver of tobacco. 'Jack, I want you to listen.' He touched his head, at the temple and pointed to a long narrow object hidden behind the low wooden garden fence. 'We use these two, an' we share Liddell's billet. Now, what could be more simple?'

'After all the dodgin' we've done, Wally, we could be caught 'ere, breakin' an enterin' — at a time when the peace officers are feelin' mean!'

'And wantin' the two of us back in the cells we escaped from,' Hexham added. And then he giggled. He also leaned over the low fence and hauled up the heavy ladder, in the horizontal position, with consummate ease. 'A little bit of risk adds a spice to life, don't it, Jack? Otherwise, we wouldn't lead the sort of life we do. So let's give it a try. I'll muscle the ladder into the vertical an' you go up it. Right?'

Fender still thought this latest venture was a mad gamble, but he went along with Hexham's desires, and discovered that his partner was very capable in handling cumbersome objects. And where many a man would have an accident standing up a ladder for the first time, Hexham got behind this one and moved it up to the vertical with scarcely a scrape as it touched the house wall.

Fender's scramble up the ladder was an easy exercise by comparison. He was so keyed up, so full of himself as he ghosted into the bedroom, that he left Hexham to his own devices and knelt beside the bed, close enough to put a revolver to Liddell's temple before there was any further chance of the sleeper being disturbed.

Mike came out of a deep sleep, felt the cold touch of metal, and murmured: 'What in tarnation is happenin' this time?'

★ ★ ★

It was rather a creepy interrogation in the darkness of the corner room. Mike Liddell made one or two spritely moves which nonplussed his interrogators, and made them postpone the weight of their deliberations until he had been properly trussed and hauled up into a sitting position.

Mike was being confronted with the situation which he had least expected. A follow-up by two men whose shape denied that they were particularly agile, and who had — for certain — been under the influence of too much alcohol a mere few hours previously.

It was uncomfortable with his arms and ankles trussed, propped up with a bolster at his back, and with a man and a pointing gun lowly placed, one on either side of him.

'I tell you once again, I never went round the back of the peace office, and therefore I never saw your partner, Ben Trine, after he walked out of the cell. I'd like to know how he got on, for my own peace of mind. Seein' as how I let him go first, when the unknown fellow pushed the key under the door. One thing I can tell you. The key was not put through by any friend of mine.

'Now, can you tell me any reason why an unknown man should try to spring the likes of you two, or Trine, out of jail?'

Hexham yawned. Holding up the revolver at the menacing angle was beginning to make him wish he had never clambered up the ladder in the first place. Jack Fender was in no better state.

The latter said: 'Would we be here, before dawn, askin' you a lot of fool questions if we knew things like that? Shucks, guess we have friends, here and there. So, what did you do with yourself? After you got out?'

'I've told it all to you, once, Jack. What good would it do to repeat it all? Haven't you heard enough?'

Mike recapped on the highlights of his protracted efforts since leaving the office. He took a deep breath at the end, and followed up non-stop with a question of his own. 'Tell me one thing, boys. Do you three, Ben and your two selves have a reward ridin' on your heads?'

Fender swore. Hexham wagged his misshapen head, and growled in a low key. 'Why do you ask that?'

Mike sniffed. 'If it's true, and the local peace office didn't know it, someone else could collect the money. Only, if you were in cells first, he'd have to let you out!'

This supposition had a startling effect upon the two gun toters. It was far easier for them to check their memories for known enemies than it was for friends. Maybe this Texan, this troubleshooter, or whatever he claimed to be, had stumbled upon the truth. The interrogators began to take their attention off Liddell and stare at one another. Mike appreciated the change, but he was still far from comfortable. When he protested at his position, they hauled him off the bed and put him on a floor mat with an old pillow behind his head.

Hexham claimed first turn on the bed, and Fender moved over by the door, taking two blankets with him. Exhaustion soon put Mike out. A new kind of worry kept the other two from making the best of a short-term opportunity.

Around six-thirty, Hexham accidentally rolled off the bed, collided with Mike, and that finished their efforts at sleeping. They undid his bonds, haranged him about doing anything stupid about getting away from them, and allowed him to go downstairs in his stockinged feet. He left another dollar in the kitchen, and a pencilled note saying farewell to Barney, and then he was back again.

Feeling mighty conspicuous, they went out by way of the ladder, one after the other and finally hauled it away in haste.

Behind a curtain, in an early-start diner, run by a Chinaman, they ate a fulsome breakfast paid for by Mike. Later, he was the one who collected their horses as well as his own palomino.

He was surprised, however, when he intimated that he wanted to go to Middleton next, that they agreed to his suggestion. The trio rode out of town, fully kitted up. Mike was just ahead of the other two, and wearing his gun belt. He reflected that his riding partners would be looking out for possible bounty hunters, as well as prowling local peace officers who had lost a lot of sleep.

8

Above all other considerations, Mike Liddell felt a sense of relief about riding clear of the new town of Riverside, and yet he found his own emotions hard to understand because there was so much unfinished business to be taken care of, and a lot of it seemed to stem from this unpredictable settlement on the banks of the turgid Pecos river.

Somewhere behind him, unless he was very much mistaken, was the girl he sought. And probably Ben Trine, the unfortunate chap who had tasted the getaway route and found it treacherous. The Dupont reception appeared to have churned up a good deal of trouble, although the newcomers themselves had never meant any harm. Would the goodwill engendered by the socialising, the free food and drink, and accommodation be worth the overall effort?

Would the Duponts be remembered as generous philanthropists, or merely as quaint people from Europe, who had a different notion of culture and an alien way of life?

From time to time, Mike looked back at his captors. Neither Hexham nor Fender were particularly athletic. Hexham had a permanant limp, and a crouching stoop such as a hunchback might assume. Fender, the Scotsman, did not appear to have any physical defects but he was clearly overweight and slow on his feet.

Mike shrugged. It took all sorts to make an outlaw group. Perhaps these two were good with six-guns. Possibly they would be quite effective on sound horses when they stayed in the saddle.

Somehow or another, he had to be rid of them. Since the cells episode, they didn't trust him, and he did not trust them. There was little he could learn from them. They did not know what had happened to Trine and seeing that they had broken out of jail themselves they did not appear to have any worthwhile plan for the future.

Mike rode and brooded. Losing touch with the English girl had seemingly begun his problems. Even now he did not blame her for apparently 'borrowing' the Beauclerc ring and substituting a ribbon of her own. He never once believed that the substitution could have been otherwise. It had been an innocent ploy used in order to bring about a meeting in the near future. One which he would have welcomed. Not knowing about the girl was almost as bad as the Trine business. Where was all this going to end? Middleton had always been a town where he had friends, where he enjoyed being, but on this particular ride it seemed as if he was riding away from his duty, away from reality.

Doubts made him push the palomino harder. Hexham and Fender were already leaking perspiration, but they did not protest. Without their leader they lacked initiative.

Mike's spurt took them almost

another mile. Down an eroded slope, through a dusty scrub-bordered shaded depression and then up and out again to a new level. There, the scrub gave way to trailside rocks like giant rugged teeth with fringes of yellowing grass where they came out of the soil.

A small park on the north side went by unnoticed, but it was to play a significant part in their present movements. When they were some twenty yards beyond it, a big round-barrelled dun horse with a white blaze between its eyes pranced out of the park and lined itself up behind them.

The man in the saddle could not have been more than forty years of age, although his swarthy face was finely wrinkled. His back was ramrod straight. He had a small brown moustache trimmed that very morning. His cranial hair was thinning and brushed across the scalp to cover bald patches. On this particular occasion he was wearing a grey flat-crowned stetson, a black shirt, a brown hide vest, denim levis and a red bandanna.

The trio ahead of him all heard the click of his gun hammers at the same time, but his clear sharp voice carried to them before they had an opportunity to do anything about it.

'I wonder if I could ask you gents to hold it right there! If you'd turn to face this way, I'd take it as a courtesy, and maybe you could lift your hands and point towards the sky to show we're all in this little meeting together! Thank you. Thank you kindly. Now that there is a real nice friendly beginning.'

The smile on the stranger's face matched the tone of his voice, except that the hard bullet tip eyes did not seem to join in. He did not look like an extra peace officer connected with the Riverside fracas, nor did he act like an ordinary hold-up man. But there was something about him. He behaved as if he had planned this meeting: almost as if he knew who he was threatening with his guns.

All three horses, having been ridden

hard for quite a distance, were restless, shifting this way and that. Mike, as near as he could, made sure that they did not screen one another from this determined gunman with the deceptive tone of voice.

Mike cleared his throat. 'If I could ask a question, sir. You seem to have us at a disadvantage. Would you care to tell us who you are, what your business is with us?'

The ready smile controlling the fine wrinkles suddenly faded. The stranger holstered his left side gun with a blur of speed. He then smiled again, almost like a conjuror at the end of a trick. He produced from the breast pocket of his shirt a slightly tarnished peace officer's star. Without looking down he contrived to pin it to his shirt.

'There now, gents. Maybe that will do instead of announcing my name. Now you know my business. In case you can't read the small print from where you are it indicates a United States federal marshal. So there now.

Having established that, I'd like for you all, one at a time, to draw your shootin' irons one at a time, and drop them to the trail. I'll tell you for why as soon as the exercise is over.

'Now, we'll start with you, sir. Mr Fender, I believe. Start with your right hand gun, an' don't do anything tricky 'cause I'm kind of nervous in my trigger finger.'

Jack Fender gasped when he heard his name. He lifted his tall undented stetson, scratched his bald patch, and then he complied with the instructions. He did not like to think that they were confronted by a federal man who knew a good deal about them. First one and then the other of his revolvers dropped into the dust.

The stranger talked encouragingly. 'And now you, sir. You with the red bandanna. You're in a different category to your riding companions, but for the moment I'll ask you to do the same.'

Maintaining a strict poker face, Mike then did as he was told. Hexham had the longest to wait, and the pointing gun seemed to fascinate him more than the others. He was quickest when it came to unloading. The stranger then gave them a smile of pure joy.

Hexham blew his nostrils, one side at once. He snorted and asked the next question. 'Does this here confrontation have to do with Riverside, or some other place, marshal?'

The stranger chuckled in his throat. He drew his left hand gun and holstered the other with a rapid movement. Next, he dipped inside his dyed hide vest and brought out three folded sheets of paper. Yellowing a little at the edges. Without looking away from his charges, he opened up the papers with one hand. Resting them against his body, he transferred the top one to the bottom.

'Now, this here printed bill says about Mr John Fender, don't it. Wanted in two counties for armed robbery, robbery with menaces which is about the same thing. And one or two lesser bits of naughtiness, adding up to a reward of fifteen hundred dollars. A nice round sum.'

He did his regular quota of laughing, before referring to the second reward notice. 'Now here is a coincidence, if you like that sort of thing. A fairly good likeness of Mr Walter Hexham, a description of his physical characteristics and then the money. The dinero, eh? Fifteen hundred dollars, once again. Exactly the same amount. Similar sort of activities, too. So you see, it's interesting for a travelling gent like myself to meet you both together. Men in my profession don't always get the chance to meet professional friends keepin' company. In a way, it makes my work that much simpler.

Mike laughed, just to break up the pattern of interrogation. 'Tell me, marshal, is *my* name and description on that other notice, by any chance?'

In asking this he wondered if he was playing into the hands of this trigger happy upholder of the law, but on this occasion at least he appeared to be in the clear.

'Why no, sir, it doesn't. The third one is a gent I already met. More interesting in some ways than present company. You see, Mr Trine is wanted for murder as well as the other crimes I've read out. A man wanted for killing rates a higher bonus. No less than three thousand dollars, and there's another consideration, too. It means a collector like me doesn't have to wet nurse him all the way to the collecting point.'

'You mean he can be taken dead or alive, marshal, ain't that so?' Mike prompted.

'I surely do, friend, I surely do. Now sir, I'd like for you to dismount, if you will, so that you can collect this hardware on the trail. You can hand up to me the guns of our friends Hexham and Fender. Then, after that it would be best if you collected your own an' kept on riding towards Middleton. We three, we'll be going back Riverside way. For a reunion, you might say, and a consultation with the local peace officer among others.'

Mike took his time in dismounting. Like the others, he had surmised that Trine was dead, and that this gunman with the irritating manner had been his killer. But if that was so, wasn't it peculiar behaviour for a federal marshal to assist in the escape of a wanted man especially to collect bounty money on him? The young Texan attempted to keep his conclusions out of his expression as he handed up the dusty six-guns and stood back again.

The stranger stacked the extra guns in his saddle pockets. He nodded for Mike to go ahead with collecting for himself and enquired what his name was.

'Why don't you ask me that the next time we meet, marshal? I'm sure it will keep.'

So saying, Mike mounted up again, turned his palomino towards the east and touched his hat. He called a general farewell to all three and rode on without looking back. For a time, he felt pleased about this latest, most unexpected development. It had ensured that he parted company with the two disgruntled gatecrashers earlier than was expected. He felt also that he had confirmation of the fate of Ben Trine. In a roundabout way, they had been told that Trine was dead, that he was about to make his last trail journey hanging limply across a saddle. The thought of it made a cold tingle go down the Texan's spine.

★ ★ ★

On a lesser hill top not more than an hour's ride out of Middleton on the Riverside trail, a still muscular figure on the back of a shaggy pinto horse surveyed distant landmarks through half-closed dark eyes shaded by the stiff brim of a dusty black flat-crowned stetson.

Johnnie Two Feathers was a full-blooded Apache who had grown used to living in white communities. At forty years of age, he worked exclusively for one Charlton Wagner, veteran banker of Middleton.

Johnnie worked as a guard, a guide and a whole lot of other specialist jobs. Mostly he protected Wagner personnel, but he also gave his skills freely where property was concerned. The Apache fringe, the poker-faced bronzed features and the smooth hairless chin nevertheless seemed to blend in with the blue shirt, denims and slack-fitting dark jacket.

The general scene looked peaceful. Not much activity, other than the movements of birds and beasts. Johnnie was in that pose for nearly ten minutes before something slightly out of the ordinary took his attention. He lifted a battered spyglass to his eye and identified one or two small dust clouds, all of which suggested a rider coming up the trail from Riverside.

This was scarcely likely to be the villain he sought. However, he decided to get down off his observation pinnacle and go close enough to converse with the newcomer, in case he had information to offer of a useful nature. Three minutes later, from a natural hiding place between masking trailside rocks, Johnnie got his first glimpse of the approaching rider and at once his mood changed. He relaxed in the saddle, made personal noises to his pinto and nudged the horse into breaking cover.

As Johnnie raised his arm in greeting, Mike Liddell recognised him and emitted an off-key war whoop.

'Johnnie, am I please to see you! Shucks, back there in Riverside all I seemed to get was surly looks and suspicious constables!'

Johnnie chuckled, as their mounts came together. 'I always thought, Mike, that for a troubleshooter you attract more than your fair share of that commodity, trouble. I don't know why you're headed for Middleton at this precise time, but we surely can use a bit of back-up if you are not too heavily involved.'

Mike shot him a shrewd glance as

they turned the horses in the direction of Middleton and started to make up ground. 'Something's happened since I took the Riverside trail out of Middleton. An accident? *Not* Ellie-May?'

Johnnie soberly shook his head. 'An incident rather than an accident, Mike. Not to the Wagners, but to an old acquaintance. Probably you'd describe him as a friend. Do you remember a federal officer who came to these parts a short while ago? Name of Jan Wilden.'

'Jan Wilden, of course I remember him. He was around when that Melindy-Lou woman and her Foreign Legion sidekick, Charles Guerin, had me on a trumped up charge at the county seat. Are you sayin' Jan's back in these parts?'

Johnnie nodded. 'Wilden had a run in with an ambusher not very far from here. A man who knew him and who thinks he is now dead. Jan survived by a miracle. What's more, he'll be glad to see you. Let's push it a bit.'

Mike at once agreed, and gave his palomino a gentle touch with the rowel.

149

9

Johnnie Two Feathers had a simple, direct way of talking and yet his descriptive powers were quite phenomenal.

'Even when he's half asleep in the saddle, Jan Wilden is a difficult man to deal with. He was gently hitting the trail by moonlight in an effort to get closer to his quarry. That's how I see it. Sometimes Jan's faculties were sharper than those of his big grey gelding. Other times the gelding did all the work.

'Anyways, this hombre up ahead of him must have been very wide awake, an' he heard the plodding horse comin' towards him. Consequently, he sets up the ambush. Some sort of sixth sense may have warned Jan, who was dozin' or possibly the grey got an inklin' of what there was ahead.

'The ambusher fired off his rifle an' took off Jan's hat. Jan then leapt from the saddle, jumpin' to his right. On that side of him was some useful cover, built up close to a fairly deep gully. As he dropped among the rocks, so a ricochet came off a rock surface.

'It altered shape, caught Jan on the low side of his rib cage, below his heart, busted a rib and also sent his marshal's badge flyin'. In order to avoid what could have been a lethal volley, he rolled further in among the rocks, and eventually did a leap into darkness. He went head first into the gully, dropped a fair way and hit his head a stunnin' blow not far from his temple.

'The blow put him out. He stayed out for quite a time, not knowin' how badly he was hurt, or whether his attacker had moved away. Eventually, he realised he was weakenin' through loss of blood, and he had to take a chance or two. No amount of whistlin' brought the grey any nearer, so he started to fire off revolver bullets at intervals of five minutes, as near as he could judge. Fortunately, I was abroad at the time, an' I heard the peculiar echo made by a gunshot in the confined space. So I came lookin'.'

'Don't tell me Ellie May was out paintin' sunrises again, with you standin' by as her guard?'

'That's about the size of things, Mike. She's a real smart girl, is Ellie May. Sunrises and sunsets are two of nature's finest times. She never tires of studying them and painting them. Ellie has poetry in her soul, an' that's for sure.'

'I know,' Mike replied simply. 'Even when you found him, you had severe difficulties, Johnnie.'

Johnnie nodded and agreed. 'Getting him up to the surface without aggravating that chest injury took a whole lot of care. And when we had him strapped up at trail level, there was still a lot to do. I had to make a travois, Mike. A frame with blankets on it. Although we were careful, Jan cried out in pain when the tail end of the travois banged on eroded stones. In fact, if we'd taken him all the way into Middleton like that he might have lost too much blood to survive.'

Mike massaged his palomino's mane, and gave it an encouraging word or two. Clearly, there was a lot more to tell and Middleton was still almost a mile away.

'Something happened to improve Jan's chances. What was it? Did you meet up with someone else mad enough to prowl about at night?'

'Not exactly, Mike. We came upon a family with a big covered wagon, parked off the trail. They had a fire going, and their dog awoke everybody through its barking. An old man and three big homely-looking sons came to see what the trouble was, toting rifles. When they heard about Jan's condition, they turned the women out of the wagon, made him up a bed on two mattresses near the tailgate and drove him all the way into town. God-fearing folk, the best kind to have around in this sort of country.

'As soon as we hit town, we called out old Sam Wagner, Charlie's brother. Abd he set up the patient in one of Charlie's rooms, and did all a sawbones could to make him comfortable and to give him a chance to get well again. I used to think he was past it.'

'Good old Doc Sam,' Mike murmured. 'I suppose he's as retired as he'll ever be in this neck of the woods. Jan *will* get well again, won't he, Johnnie?'

'I believe so, Mike. You see he was on a special job, like always and he'll want to pass on certain information to others. Even if he's incapacitated. Sam bandaged him, and doped him, but he could be conscious again by the time you get there. The local town marshal will have to be told who the patient is, but he'll open up to you when he's feelin' strong enough. I feel sure he will. Jan has confidence in you.'

Mike smiled and nodded. Maybe Jan wouldn't be so forthcoming on this occasion. Not if there was another federal officer riding the trails of Sunset County on a similar errand.

★ ★ ★

Ellie May Rondell ran a whole hundred yards at a good speed when she realised that Johnnie Two Feathers was back and that he had Mike Liddell with him.

'Did you find the man you sought, Johnnie?' she called out breathlessly, from several yards away.

'No, I wasn't that fortunate, Ellie-May,' Johnnie replied,' but I did find this hombre on the trail an' headin' this way. So I came along with him on account of Jan would likely want to see him. Don't you think so?'

Johnnie swung to the ground, and Ellie-May hugged him. Next, she hurried over to Mike. Before he could dismount, she had placed a foot over his boot and jumped up behind him, using his arm as a lever. Mike squirmed about and kissed her on the cheek.

'On account of Jan and his setback, I'd almost forgotten about you and the goings on in Riverside. Did it all go well, Mike?'

Mike gave a big shrug of resignation. 'The Duponts have problems, Ellie, and some of them rubbed off on me. But nothing so serious as this attack on Jan. He hasn't had a relapse or anything since Johnnie came away, has he?'

'No, nothing like that has happened, but he doesn't look at all well to me. I can't make out whether Sam has doped him too much, or if he's lost so much blood that he is comatose. Know what I mean?'

Johnnie took control of the two horses. Ellie took Mike by the hand and walked him indoors. Mike forcibly stopped her, so that he could take off his boots. The girl knelt down and helped him. Jan Wilden was slightly propped up in a wide single bed in one of the back bedrooms on the ground floor. The window was open, and also the door.

Maria Serano, Charlie Wagner's elderly Mexican housekeeper, was seated on an upright chair just inside the room. She was still, and her head was dropping. Hand in hand, Ellie and Mike tiptoed past Maria and stood together not far from the bed.

Most of Wilden's long sleek silver hair was hidden by a bandage draped about his head to help the recovery of the cuts and swollen bruise just behind his temple. Under the snowy covers, the peace officer looked more bulky than usual. The doctor had strapped his left arm to his body to give support to the broken rib. Jan was titled slightly towards his right side. His breathing, as he slept, was noisy and yet he seemed restless.

Maria roused herself, fought off the drowsiness of early afternoon, and greeted Mike in a whisper. She conducted the two of them out of the room. In an empty bedroom, she explained the present position.

'The loss of blood is bothering the

doctor. Señor Sam, he says the marshal must not be disturbed for another hour and a half, unless he murmurs about water.'

Maria was so concerned that she talked in Spanish rather than English. Fortunately, both her listeners knew enough of Spanish to understand her. Ellie offered to give Maria a spell off, as the bedside watcher, but the old woman courteously refused.

Ellie took Mike into the dining room. There, they found the brothers Wagner. Charlton, the banker, was lolling back in a lounging chair, a dressing gown wrapped round him, his feet on a foot stool. A small cigar in an ivory holder had gone out. He had ceased to be interested in the view beyond the window, having dropped off to sleep. Samuel, the doctor, who was five years older, had slumped into a deeper sleep in a rocking chair. His bald head lolled over one shoulder. His pince nez had been removed from his bulbous nose and were currently clipped on the index finger of his left hand.

Ellie gestured towards the table. It was laden with the remains of three courses of food. In addition, there was wine of two varieties and three types of fruit juice. Mike shook his head, at first. He was hungry but at the same time too thirsty to contemplate food.

The girl pressed him to a large beaker of mixed fruit juice, poured out for him a glass of his favourite wine, and conducted him into the empty lounge, where he stretched out at once on the long broad settee.

'Call me in one and a half hours, sweetie,' he murmured, his eyes already closed.

Almost at once, he started to drift off into sleep. Ellie knelt beside him, kissed her finger and lightly touched it to his lips. He touched her hand. When he was sleeping soundly, she withdrew her hand and curled up on a thick bearskin close by.

Instinctively, she knew that he had had a bad time in Riverside. Later, he would tell her just how bad. She knew without being told that due to this murderous attack on Jan Wilden, Mike was likely to take on a good deal more responsibility than was rightfully his. She hoped he would always be lucky in his efforts to protect others.

★   ★   ★

Two hours had gone by when Mike slowly came back to consciousness. He blinked his eyes, noticed his whereabouts and frowned, as his thoughts centred on Jan Wilden. Distantly, there was a clock ticking, and somewhere else in the house two people were talking earnestly.

Mike rose to his feet and tiptoed back towards the wounded man's bedroom. The door was still ajar. Only Ellie-May was in the room. She had been conversing with Jan, who looked pale in spite of his weathered complexion. There was a feverishness about his eyes and yet he seemed to have full

160

control of his senses.

'There you are, Ellie-May. I've signed it. You take charge of it for the time being. Hey, would you believe he's here! Sit down, Mike, and listen, please. The dope old Sam gave me keeps taking me out an' I may not have a lot of time before I lose consciousness again.'

Mike planted himself on an upright chair, his expression showing his concern abot Jan's weakness. 'It's good to see you, Jan, even when you're in bad shape. If only I'd ridden up that trail from Riverside a bit sooner, I could maybe have saved you from the ambusher.'

Jan nodded and smiled. He gestured with his workable hand, the right. 'Michael, there are few men a chap in my profession can unburden himself to. There are things I have to tell you. I came south into New Mexico territory on the trail of a villain who ought to have been taken out a long time ago. He operates under various names, but the one he uses mostly is Rufus Volk. He's a man hunter, and he takes some stopping. He'll go against a man on the run, and other times he'll take on an assignment as an assassin. Volk has to be stopped. A bullet is the only thing likely to halt him.

'His trail has not been easy to follow, but he's here. Movin' around in Sunset County. An' that ain't healthy for the folks who live here. It really needs a man who can think like him to stop him. You ought to alert that undertaking agency. Earl Martin and his boys. They might be able to outsmart him, given a bit of luck.

'I don't want to dwell on his viciousness in front of Ellie-May. Take that as said. Now, I heard on the grapevine that he was headed into Sunset County to do a special job. He was supposed to be joining a couple of smart villains who have operated in these parts before. A man and a woman. The woman is said to be of Latin extraction. Either French or

Spanish. And the man is from Europe, too. He has a military background. The word is that he has changed his appearance, and the woman is quite adept at disguises.'

Mike groaned. He started to shake his head, having already made up his mind about the identities of the two people being described.

'Charles Guerin and Manuela Sanchez, *again*?'

Jan nodded very decidedly. He was beginning to show signs of drowsiness. Ellie-May, whose mind was primarily on him, dabbed his brow with a white cloth. She was biting her lip in anxiety, her alert blue eyes darting from one man to the other.

'You know her, then. Manuela Sanchez. Sometimes she becomes Melindy-Lou. She has worked as a trapeze artist. So, even though she's pressing forty years of age, she's fit and strong. Or, Marie-Louise. Which suggests she's fluent in French and Spanish, as well as English.

'A big girl, by any standards. Mexican and French Canadian parents. An hour glass figure. A Syrian nose. Long, shapely legs. Good teeth. Dark brown hair. May have had dealings with a knife thrower.'

'You know your women, Jan. No one can take that away from you,' Mike remarked quietly.

Jan acknowledged. His eyelids started to droop. Ellie mimed for Mike to let him doze off. The worried young Texan agreed.

Jan slept. Mike and Ellie came out, hand in hand. The Wagner brothers had gone out for a walk. Mike seated himself in the empty rocker, where Ellie joined him.

'I need to know the identity of his partner, little squaw.'

'Jan is a loner, as you know. He didn't have a partner. He came from Colorado alone. Why did you think he had a partner?'

'Bedause I met a man on trail further south, who pinned a federal officer's badge to his shirt. He must be Jan's ambusher, the assassin. If so, he's killed one man already in this county. I don't like this development, Ellie. I'm going to need help!'

'Thank goodness we found out in time, Mike,' Ellie whispered, her head pressed against his chest.

10

Presently, Ellie-May went away to check that the Lehmann shop was being properly run, and that those temporarily in charge of it were coping well.

Mike was very fond of Ellie, but on this occasion he was glad to be on his own for a short while to think out the colossal implications of what he had learned about two old enemies of the Beauclercs and this new one, the assassin and bounty hunter, who had already made his presence felt during his brief stay in the county.

Manuela Sanchez and Charles Guerin had banded together in an all out effort to make money out of la Baronne de Beauclerc. In fact, the lady in question had been kidnapped and only rescued with great difficulty. Guerin had been wounded and in custody, but during a spell when Mike was away from Sundown and the chateau, the Sanchez woman had masqueraded as la Baronne and taken Guerin out of custody. At the same time, she had brought a defaming case against Mike Liddell which had caused him a great deal of trouble and proved very frustrating.

At the end of that last clash, Sanchez and Guerin had escaped over the border with Texas. Now, it seemed they were back, eager and ready to pit their wits and skills once again against the Beauclerc household and the family fortune.

Mike paused, rubbed out the butt of a small cigar, and started pacing again in his stockinged feet. He knew beyond a shadow of doubt that both the Sanchez woman and the ex-*legionnaire* officer had a deep and abiding hatred of all things Beauclerc. Hence this coming together with a most notorious assassin from north of the border. So far as he knew, Rufus Volk was known to be a slippery customer. Mike could not be sure that he would stay down Riverside way.

For a time, he did not know what to do for the best. The Beauclerc household in Sundown City was the permanent home of several people, not just la Baronne. Moreover, the house was full of priceless relics and artifacts. And since the Lehmann shop in Middleton had been more or less taken over by la Baronne, after the demise of the previous owner, there was a distinct possibility that the shop's contents were at risk, too.

Personnel or property? Which was most important? Or, should he simply alert the chateau, and go after the new threat, namely the assassin, Volk?

Long experience made him discard the latter notion. Volk would turn up of his own accord. The obvious thing to do was make contact by telegraph. He had dollars in his pocket and a fair notion as to whom should be contacted. So, after leaving a message with the stable boy, he set off on foot for town and began composing his messages as he went.

The first one was to Town Marshal Abel Smith, the stiff-legged peace officer in charge of Sundown, where the Beauclerc residence was. It read:

Take note Federal Marshal Jan Wilden newly arrived Middleton is incapacitated. Contact Wagner.
                    Mike Liddell,
                    Middleton.

The second one was to La Baronne de Beauclerc, also in Sundown. It read:

Attending other business in Middleton. May return soon. Any new unresolved business visitors your end? Reply.
                    Mike Liddell.

The third was to the county sheriff, Sunrise.

Note Federal Marshal Jan Wilden ambushed incapacitated Middleton-Riverside area.

A fourth was to the new Town Marshal of Riverside, informing him of Mike Liddell's presence in Middleton, and that he was in close liaison with Federal Marshal Jan Wilden who was incapacitated.

Having arranged for these to be sent, Mike said he would call back in the hour to check on any return messages. Meanwhile, in the private quarters at the back of the Lehmann shop, Ellie made him a fresh meal while he told her a little of the goings on at the Dupont residence.

At the end of the meal, he repeated to her the descriptions of the two Dutch miniatures and the small silver salver, which Isabel Valero had said were missing.

'If anyone brings in anything of a suspect nature, Ellie, be careful. You could be dealing with thieves we don't know about yet, or someone in touch with this Volk character. Or even a person acting for Sanchez or Guerin. Come to think of it, I don't know how

I'm goin' to be able to protect all of you in the future.

'And there's another character not accounted for. One Jean-Jacques Perçot, who came over from France with the Dupont family. He had worked for the Dupont bank, prior to coming overseas. When I left Riverside, he was missing. Certain puzzling eventualities suggested that he might have sold off a few invitations to the Dupont reception to undesirable strangers for personal gain. Hell, what a mess the decent folk of this small county are getting themselves into!'

The bell rang in the shop, indicating the arrival of a customer. Harry Wakeford, the boy who lived near, came in. He began to chuckle to himself. Mike found out why shortly afterwards when Johnnie Two Feathers' indescribable chuckle indicated that the Indian had entered the shop without the usual bell sounding.

'Howdy, Mike. Howdy, Ellie,' young Harry remarked excitedly. 'Mr Wagner was talkin' to the telegraph clerk when I came by. The clerk asked where you were, and Mr Wagner offered to deliver two messages to you. Charlie, I mean, Mr Wagner, asked me to bring them along here because they're urgent. Mr Wagner will be here in a minute, Mike.'

Mike accepted them and moved aside from the others. He had been anticipating replies, but now he had a premonition, an instinct, that another setback had occurred. Perhaps forebodings were a proper part of his job as a troubleshooter, but he found them hard to take.

The first reply was from La Baronne. She intimated in her own words that there had been no visitors at all to the chateau. She added her regards, and promised to let him know of any change in the present situation.

He breathed out in relief. 'No trouble at the chateau. But what about this other message? It's from the new town, Riverside. Town Marshal van Dune acknowledges, and he says 'Now imperative Mike Liddell returns immediately to Riverside due to death of young female visitor to Dupont reception.''

Mike groaned and turned the messages over to Ellie, who went through the motions of reading them.

'It doesn't say who the young lady is, Mike, but I think you could make a shrewd guess. Am I right?'

'You are right, Ellie. I have this gut feeling that the lady in question did not die a natural death. And it may very well turn out to be a young person with an English accent. One I was fortunate enough to become acquainted with. I tried to find her before I came away, but I never did find the place where she was staying.'

'Is there anything else bothering you, Mike?' Johnnie asked. 'Anything new?'

Mike nodded. 'It seems very likely that the federal marshal I met before you contacted me was none other than Jan Wilden's ambusher, wearin' Jan's star. See what I mean, Johnnie?'

The Indian nodded. The way his

restless eyes were shifting about revealed that he was weighing up the situation with extreme care.

Ellie added: 'And Jan was sayin' that the villain in question, Rufus Volk, was headed into this county to link up with two known enemies of the Beauclerc residence. Manuela Sanchez and Charles Guerin.'

Johnnie whistled. 'Do you think he'll still be bluffin' it out in Riverside, makin' out he's a federal marshal?'

They all seated themselves: some on chairs, others on a settee and one who leaned against the counter.

'If he is, we'll be able to get close to him and keep a watch on him,' Mike remarked, 'but I think he only assumed the guise of a federal man to pick up the reward cash more easily on Trine and the other two. If he drops out of circulation, he could do a lot of damage as not many people know what he looks like.'

'If you could describe him, Mike, I could sketch him,' Ellie offered.

At that moment, the dapper portly figure of the bank president came briskly through the outer door. He looked warm in his customary stiff collar, grey coat and dark trousers. Already he had removed his topper, to keep his brow cool.

'Capital,' Charlie remarked, subsiding into a chair vacated by his granddaughter, 'always make use of the family talents. Sorry if I've taken a long time.'

Ellie patiently went through the items which had just been discussed. It gave the breathless banker time to recover, as well an opportunity to polish his steamed-up monocle. By the time Charlton had heard it all, his rubicund face had altered shape. His jowl appeared to have grown heavier. His shoulders had also rounded a little. He cleared his throat.

'Well, Mike, you won't hesitate to tell me if there's anything I can do, apart from supply obvious funds for another nasty incursion against the lives and property of our friends. Do you have anything in mind, young man?'

'No obvious plan, as yet, Charlie,' Mike admitted. 'But if you could bribe your best telegraph clerk to stay on the job a bit longer, an' keep his wits about him, that might help. One other thing. We need manpower. Someone ought to send a telegraph message to Earl Martin. Tell him to be on the alert for trouble, and to come as far as Middleton as soon as possible.

'Either Ellie or Johnnie could be on hand to bring him and his boys up to date, and to pass on any urgent information as to where they can be best employed.'

The discussion went on for another five minutes. After that, it was decided to close the store early. Johnnie and Ellie went along with Mike, who was anxious to get back to the painting salon so that the assassin's likeness could be reproduced.

Harry Wakeford saw to the locking up, while Charlton Wagner took a short rest on a bench in the back garden before making the return journey to his hacienda.

The rapport between Mike and Ellie made the composing of Volk's likeness an interesting exercise. The first effort was in full face, clearly showing his wrinkled face, the small moustache which masked his mouth and the deadly look in his eyes. The second showed a profile, where his curling brows showed up, and his low prominent forehead. His slightly misshapen nose took a few efforts to get it to Mike's satisfaction. At length, however, he stepped back and admired the result.

'He lifted his hat once to scratch his head. He has dark, thinning hair, brushed across from left to right. He's swarthy, and he sits like a ramrod in the saddle.'

Johnnie gave up whistling through his teeth. 'They come in all shapes and sizes. Villains, I mean.'

Jan Wilden was still sleeping when they enquired, and Doc Wagner had nothing further to report about his general condition. In the stable, Ellie, Johnnie and Mike said their farewells.

As he walked his palomino across the paddock, Mike had a last piece of information to pass on. 'Volk rides a round-barrelled dun gelding with a white blaze.'

'I'll be lookin' for him' Johnnie promised.

Ellie's lip trembled at the last minute. 'Hey, Mike, no more casualties, huh? An' keep in touch!'

'I'll be with you when I can, folks, an' I don't need any likeness of you two. Adios!'

As he rode away, he had second thoughts about likenesses. After all, for a lonely man who spent many hours in the saddle, the likeness of a affection-ate, pretty young girl would be heart warming, at times.

11

Mike rode until dusk. Bearing in mind the ambush of the previous day (or was it two days) he then reined in, found a secluded piece of ground on which to camp and hurriedly prepared a trailside meal. He found that his appetite had in no way suffered and soon he was casting around for some sort of distraction before attempting to sleep.

Mental theorising did him no good at all. He knew he had pressing problems ahead of him, but trying to work out how he would act in uncertain circumstances did not do him any good. If thinking was useless, then he had to try something of a more physical nature. His first improvised diversion was to climb a tree. A nearby stunted oak provided the challenge and, wearing a pair of scuffed mocassins, he rose to a height where branches would no longer support him, and then started back down again.

As his mind still seemed to be overactive, he took on a rocky outcrop. Even in the gloom, he clambered up a half of an old talus slope without serious difficulty and only abandoned his task when displaced soil began to whisper on its way down to a lower level.

Only a few small stones were tempted to move by his presence: nevertheless, extreme prudence was called for on account of his being entirely alone and with no known chance of assistance in the event of an accident.

He was only in his bedroll for ten minutes before sleep claimed him, and when he awoke the following morning he did it slowly; pleasantly aware of the twittering birds, the scudding by of light clouds and fresh earthy smells permeating the atmosphere.

He started to think about people. Ellie May. Jan Wilden. Johnnie Two

Feathers. The hostile peace officers in Riverside, and the enigmatic English girl who had been his close companion for so brief a time. He was frowning as he fried his bacon, catfooting round the fire avoiding the coffee pot with its lifting lid.

Within a half hour, he was saddled up and on his way.

He started to approach Riverside with mixed feelings towards eleven o'clock. The palomino had slowed down, as if it also was not particularly keen to renew acquaintance with the waterside settlement. As he rode down the intersection which led to the main thoroughfare and the peace office, strolling men and women began to take notice of him. However, he did nothing to draw attention to himself, and soon he was dismounting at the hitchrail which had been badly chewed in the past by impatient horses left tied up for too long.

Deputy Jake Read was in the office on his own. Mike went in quickly. As he did so, the deputy hastily removed a pair of reading glasses from half way up his nose and pushed aside a month old newspaper.

'Oh, it's you, I see. Mike Liddell. Well, I suppose you didn't waste any time getting here after the message was delivered.'

Mike touched his hat and swayed on his boot heels. 'A fair assessment of my efforts to get here, deputy. As a matter of fact, I slept in the open last night. I doubt if you did the same, but you do look as if you slept in your suit. Now, pressing business. But before we start you could answer me a few questions.

'Do you have Hexham an' Fender here in custody?'

Read rocked to his feet, pushed back the swivel chair and started to buckle on his gun belt. 'Nope, we don't have them any more. They was brought in by the federal officer, along with the body of Ben Trine. Trine went to be fitted for a box. The others were hustled away under escort, headed for the county seat. I ain't sure that you yourself don't have charges to answer, so I wouldn't act like you owned the place. Not yet a while!'

From his pocket Mike produced Jan Wilden's letter of authority. Grudgingly, Read reseated himself and replaced the reading spectacles on his nose. Not waiting for him to read the missive through, Mike then quoted the gist of it from memory.

''I, Jan Wilden, United States Federal Marshal, am incapacitated in the town of Middleton. Unfortunately, I shall not be fit enough to carry out the task I had set myself, on entering this county. In brief, it concerns the doings of a known assassin, sometimes known as Rufus Volk, who came into Sunset for the express purpose of linking up with two other known villains, Charles Guerin and Manuella Sanchez, who are already known to the county sheriff and others.

'Volk is extremely dangerous. No peace officer is to trust him. It is believed that he is masquerading as a federal officer and possibly using my badge. In special need of protection are Madame la Baronne de Beauclerc, respected citizen of Sundown City, and certain other well to do people known to her, and to the bearer of this message, Michael Liddell.

'The said Michael Liddell moves against Volk and the other villains whose names are here given with my full authority and confidence. All local peace officers should give him all the help he needs at any time. Yours dutifully, Jan Wilden. Etc.''

When the enormity of this revelation had struck Read, he seemed incapable of looking up. Mike, therefore, gently extracted the letter from his fingers and rested himself on the corner of the desk.

'So now you know, deputy. I need to be put in touch with Henry van Dune, and the deceased young female visitor without further delay. Is she still at the Dutch villa?'

Read shook his head. 'She's been

moved to a private room in the doctor's house. Someone from the Dupont residence is expected this afternoon to give instructions about the burial. As it happens, the marshal is over at the doc's right now.'

Question upon question flooded to the forefront of the young Texan's mind. Somehow, he managed to restrain himself, however, and they reached Doctor Walter Bergerac's detached house at the west end of Second Street some five minutes later.

Bergerac was an imposing figure. Although he was in his late fifties his thick black hair, parted down the middle, made him seem at least ten years younger. He assessed his visitors over pince nez with a finger and thumb buried deeply into a waistcoat pocket, as if he wanted to take snuff from it.

'Good day to you, doctor. Michael Liddell of Sundown City, on the delicate matter of deceased female visitor. I was sent for.'

Mike took off his hat, stood to one

side to allow Deputy Read through the door and was the first to see Marshal van Dune emerge from another door, scratching his pink scalp and sniffing. On seeing who it was, the marshal's surly face brightened and then reflected belligerence. He felt around for his gun belt, recollected that he was not wearing it, and began to aim his index finger in Mike's direction.

On impulse, Mike turned his back upon the marshal. He handed the Wilden letter over to the deputy, and told him what to do with it.

'Here, deputy. Take your head man aside and explain how the impostor has made a complete fool of him, and then be good enough to let me have the letter back.'

Mike side-stepped, propelled the deputy in the direction of the irate and baffled marshal, and at once engaged the doctor in further conversation. Bergerac, who had no particular liking for the town peace officers, drew Mike into another room and stepped closer, expecting an explanation of some sort.

Mike told him of Jan Wilden's fate, the gist of the letter, and some details about Rufus Volk, who had already been paid out on the say-so of the marshal and the town lawyer, currently the mayor.

'How well do you know Sam Wagner?' Bergerac asked.

Mike explained the close affinity between the Wagners and the Beauclerc menage, and added some details about how old Sam was tending the stricken federal officer. Bergerac had known the Wagners for many years, and everything Mike said about the Middleton family reinforced the confidence the doctor had in him.

Indicating a padded chair, the doctor gestured for Mike to be seated. After a moment's hesitation, the young man complied.

'I'm very sorry about Miss Rowena Jane Randolph, Michael. I mention this because although she was in this area for only a short time I believe you came to know her.'

Mike winced. Was that her name, then? Rowena Jane Randolph. He was not thinking too clearly at the time, so he asked a question.

'How did you know? I mean what was the connection, doctor?'

'Your ring, of course. As soon as the young lady's body was put into my care I started to put together the things I could find out about her, as well as the cause of death. If you are still keen to see her remains, we ought to do it fairly soon. We don't want to be disturbed, of course. I have to tell you she died by a knife thrust, just under the heart. It isn't likely that she suffered much pain. In fact, I can't be sure, strictly speaking, whether she was wide awake or not.

'Let's go in, before van Dune comes through. I'm sure his presence will upset you.'

The curtains were drawn in the small tastefully furnished room beyond. The still figure was laid out on a low trolley with a wheel base and covered with a white sheet. Bergerac stepped to the head, raised his brows and Mike nodded. Underneath, the youthful female figure was draped in a white gown.

The dimples were just visible in the cheeks, due to a half smile. The expression seemed incongruous at first, bearing in mind that she had died as a result of a stab wound. Mike found himself wondering if a skilled doctor could change a dead person's expression, but he dismissed that idea as impossible.

To stop his pent-up emotions from getting the better of him, Mike talked as he looked.

'All the time I was dancing with her at the Dupont reception, I had no clear idea of her appearance, except that I knew she was nicely proportioned and that she moved easily. All the time she had on a crinoline type gown, a mask and a wig. So although I felt I knew her well, I couldn't really have described her. And now I can't even hear her distinctive voice again. Why should anyone want to kill her, doctor?'

'That will have to remain a mystery, Michael. She had a room in an annexe belonging to a house known locally as the Dutch house. One would think she had been travelling a lot, an' when the event was over she had the habit of retiring into her room and putting up a sign which said she didn't want to be disturbed. Whether she carried expensive jewelry with her, none of us can tell. I've tried once or twice to contact the lady she works for. She was the travelling companion, you see, to her employer, a French lady of independent means. One Mademoiselle Stephanie Louise Leduc. But Miss Leduc seems to be even more retiring than Miss Randolph was.

'She's the one who is supposed to be coming over here to give us instructions about the burial, but just when she'll arrive, I really don't know.'

Mike nodded. With an effort he pulled his steadfast gaze away from the still intriguing head and shoulders. He had no doubts about this being his companion of the dance. In fact, he had noticed a small detail, a tiny brown mole above the right breast, and there was something special about the mouth, too.

'I never even knew what colour her eyes were, but it's good to know her hair was like it is, fine as silk and dark almost enough to be black.'

Without knowing it, the tone of his voice was betraying the depth of his feeling. Bergerac drew him away and recovered the still figure. In the adjacent room, Mike learned a few more facts. The doctor opened a drawer above his desk and brought out two objects from it. A ring and a letter. As he pushed them towards his visitor, he remarked: 'Her eyes were a delicate shade of green. Very fetching, they must have been in life.

'You'd better keep your ring. No one can really deny your right to it, especially as your name is inscribed on the inner side. Michael Bonnard Liddell. A name to conjure with. I discovered it when I put the ring under my magnifying glass.'

'Thank you, doctor. Losing it put me under a lot of pressure, especially as a few valuable items went missing at the reception. I knew she had it, of course.' His tenseness temporarily left him, as he explained. 'She had a bruised hand, due to a fall or something during a horse riding session. And I bruised it by gripping her hand too tightly during the dance. I put the ring in my bolero pocket. I was dressed up as a toreador for the evening, you see. When I wanted to prove my identity with the ring it had gone. In its place was a short length of ribbon which she had been wearing in her hair. *I* wanted to meet her again, and she had the same idea. May I ask where the ring was when you found it?'

Mike absently brought a small cigar from his pocket. Bergerac declined to take one, himself, but provided a match stick instead.

'There was no mystery about where she had it. She was wearing it on the longest finger of her right hand. It was a fairly good fit, too. If I hadn't taken it off when I did, I doubt it would have been possible to remove in the ordinary course of events.'

Mike whistled gently, filling much of the room with cigar smoke.

'How, how was she clad when the attack took place?'

The tension was back in him again. Bergerac smiled, transforming his otherwise unresponsive features. He moved over to the window and opened it. 'She was lightly clad. She might have been lying down when the assailant attacked her. There was some blood, but I cleaned it up when I closed her eyes.'

It was an imposing ring whatever the time of day. Solid, rich-looking, with the big Beauclerc 'B' and the circle embossed upon it for anyone to see. Many people knew of it, and its significance in Sunset County. Mike used it like a passport, or a calling card.

Although his senses and his emotions had taken a number of shocks already since his arrival, a few new thoughts mulling about in his head were disturbing enough to make him rise to his feet without being aware of it.

'If you've come to a shattering conclusion, Mike, perhaps you ought to tell me what it is,' Bergerac prompted calmly. 'It's clear to me that this young lady meant an awful lot to you, even on such a brief acquaintance. Now, what was it?'

Mike groaned. 'When we danced, we talked. I intimated that I was not a Beauclerc, that is, a rich titled person. And Miss Randolph, she did the same. I was wondering, if she didn't have a lot of valuables of her own, why was she attacked? And my thoughts came back to the ring.

'The man who attacked Jan Wilden came into this county to team up with two other villains for the purpose of mounting an attack or attacks upon the Beauclerc household and Beauclerc property . . . '

'And you believe he saw the exclusive

194

Beauclerc ring on Miss Randolph's finger,' the doctor put in, 'and she was slain because she was wearing it. A shattering conclusion for a young man emotionally involved with the victim!'

Mike had heard everything Bergerac said, and yet his thoughts were a little way beyond the present conversation. Could it have been Rufus Volk who had attacked her? Or Sanchez, or Guerin? Or was it someone else with a motive as yet unknown?

While he was still deliberating, van Dune banged upon the door with calloused knuckles and blundered into the room. This precipitate action caused Mike to pocket the letter and to work the all-important ring onto his finger.

12

Henry van Dune would have made a good rugby player if that peculiar robust male team game had been known in the U.S. of A., in his time.

Mike Liddell shifted first to one side and then to the other, seeking a way past the crestfallen official who just a day or so earlier had shown him anything but sympathy and fair treatment. Some men are more difficult when in a mood to be humble than they are when aggressive. Van Dune was one of these. He moved with Mike and prevented his going by.

'Mr Liddell, you didn't get a fair crack of the whip back there at the Dupont place. For that reason, I want to express my sorrow. I needed a rebuke. If Federal Marshal Wilden has confidence in you, then I ought at least to help you in any way I can. Here's your letter of reference. I hope you get all the assistance you need without having to show it any more. Me, and my team, we'll put ourselves at your service an' if you're in telegraphic touch with Mr Wilden I hope you'll tell him so. I hope he gets well again without too much of a delay, either. Now, is there any line of enquiry you'd like to see followed up? Anything for us to make a start on?'

Instead of deliberately barging past this rather stolid peace-keeper Mike forced himself to be patient. He acknowledged a few mimed hints from Deputy Read, who was behind the marshal's back, suggesting that the deputy had finally managed to put the marshal in his place, at last.

'All right, marshal. For my part, I'm going to seek out Miss Randolph's employer, the French person she came to town with. As for your enquiries, I think you should be seeking out the man who came here makin' out to be a federal officer, and who helped himself to bounty money concerning the late Ben Trine, and the two other men who were in cells the same time as I was.'

Van Dune blinked, nodded heavily and frowned, as he recollected that Trine was already buried, and that Hexham and Fender had been sent to the safer quarters in the county seat, with an escort.

'Don't be afraid to use the telegraph, marshal. In a short time, sketches will be available throughout the peace offices of the county, showin' the actual features of one Rufus Volk, assassin and bounty hunter. *You* won't need to wait for the particulars because you were around when Volk was paid out for releasin' and shootin' Trine, etc.'

Van Dune rolled his shoulders and appeared to shrink within his clothes. 'But are you absolutely sure that was Volk, the killer?'

'I've met him. You've met him. We are actin' on the say-so of Jan Wilden. He followed him here from Colorado. So there's no doubt. Now, if you'll allow me, I've got my own enquiries to make.'

Van Dune backed off to one side, and pushed Read away in the opposite direction, but Mike delayed long enough to exchange a few more courteous words with the doctor before leaving the building.

Two things were uppermost in his mind as he stepped clear of the well-kept building. One was the letter in his pocket, and the other was concerning the palomino, left hitched outside the peace office, where it would also be reduced to nibbling the woodwork. Thought of nibbled woodwork gave him an empty feeling in the pit of his stomach. He was beginning to think that action, lethal action in fact, was not far away. That consideration, and the time of day was sharpening his own appetite.

His long legs soon carried him back to the front of the peace office, where the high-stepping light-coloured horse at once acknowledged him. Constable Bluey Dunstable's homely features appeared at the fly-specked window, but the hollow-eyed Australian policeman withdrew again, no doubt hoping that Mike would not be entering the office.

The Texan, in fact, checked that the palomino had drunk from the nearby water trough. He then adjusted the grip of the saddle and mounted up. Food smells were teasing his nostrils from either direction. The memory of an earlier meal in a Chinese diner prompted him where to go, and it was thither that he went. As he entered the diner, the palomino protested by stamping the ground and kicking up a groove of dirt.

The proprietor followed him up the long narrow restaurant to the secluded curtained-off area, and there they studied a well-headed, well-lubricated rancher type who had finished his meal and fallen asleep with his two-gallon stetson still in place. Mike looked at the small Chinese and the two of them shrugged delicately. Mike grinned, and between them they hoisted the dozing man to his feet and walked him through the common table area with his trailing booted feet scoring a pace every now and then.

Thus ejected, the rancher protested a bit as the change of air on the sidewalk revived him, but the ejectors ignored him. Back in the curtained area, a small Chinese female was making off with the dirty dishes. Mike gave his order, asked if the drunk had paid for his meal and was assured that the fellow had paid in advance.

Alone at last with his thoughts and the letter which he had not read, Mike slumped. He removed his stetson, slackened off his bright red bandanna, and produced the letter from the envelope. At once, he was intrigued. The date inside showed that it had been written the previous autumn. The inside address was Rue Hortense, Quebec, Canada. It was written in French, a language which he had learned as a boy while his folks were still alive, in the neighbouring state of Texas.

Ma Chere Stephanie,
Thank you for your charming letter, so welcome, all the way from Lille, France. So nice to renew acquaintance with you, and to know that you will be visiting *le Canada* next spring!

Hearing from you makes me yearn for my beloved France — Paris in particular. However, here I am and here I must stay. You will be welcome in my home at any time. When you come stay as long as you are able. And then, if you have more time, go south into *les États-Unis* and visit my dear cousin, Madeleine, la Baronne de Beauclerc. I fear she will be lonely for her own kind, widowed as she is, since her father-in-law, Monsieur le Comte died.

I have not corresponded with Madeleine for a little time, but she would be delighted to see you, and would make you welcome.

My deepest, warm regards.
Your friend for all time,
Helen Arnot.

Michael read the letter through twice, and then returned it to the envelope which smelled faintly of the perfume he associated with Rowena Jane. It seemed strange that the Randolph girl should have this letter, probably addressed to her employer, in her possession.

However, it was quite a revealing bit of information and it showed a tie-up between the Mademoiselle Leduc from Lille, France, and Mike's employer, Madeleine.

Recent revelations seemed to suggest that Madeleine was due for desirable visitors, as well as undesirables of the calibre of Volk, Sanchez and Guerin. What a pity that the beautiful Rowena Jane had not survived long enough to make the acquaintance of Madeleine, and the other people at the Beauclerc chateau whom Michael had come to think of as his family. Had it been the other way round, had Mademoiselle Leduc died suddenly and Miss Randolph survived, Mike felt sure that Madeleine would have found a permanent place for the English girl at the Beauclerc house, with very little prompting.

The food came, and he put aside the revealing letter which the thoughtful doctor had brought to his notice. All through three succulent courses, he brooded over past events and what his own future movements ought to be.

In the forefront of his mind, a visit to the Duponts.

★　★　★

Enriquez Alfredo Anton, the Duponts' new Spanish butler, had once worked for a titled house south of the border in Mexico. Consequently, Enriquez had the style, and the style suited a family freshly away from the well mannered servants of la Belle France.

Mike left his protesting yellow horse a few yards down the approach road to the stylish residence and walked up to the main entrance, intent upon being admitted to the presence of someone in authority.

Enriquez answered the bell, was greeted in good cowpuncher English which failed to get a laugh out of the butler and caused Mike to be dismissed peremptorily. Mike called after the retiring portly figure a rude word which a Parisian gustersnipe might have used on a slow-moving *agent-de-police* and was rather surprised when it provoked no sort of reaction whatsoever.

He waited for five minutes, and then rang again. This time, he positioned himself behind a few potted shrubs and called out to the suspicious silver-haired butler in Spanish.

Mike prattled on about the toreador costume which he had left in a hedge during a previous visit. he added that it had been worn by one of the most formidable bullfighters in Barcelona at one time, and when he was sure that he had the full attention of the Mexican door opener, he stepped from cover, flashed all his teeth in a big smile and bowed from the hips. His effort had the required effect.

'*Buenas tardes*, what can I do for you, *Señor*?'

'Señor Mike Liddell. I am not here to collect the toreador costume. You, or one of the other persons may keep it. I am here to make contact with a young French lady. One of the visitors for the reception. Mademoiselle Stephanie Louise Leduc. Do you think it would be convenient to see her now?'

Enriquez murmured that it would be very difficult. He requested that Mike should be seated in the foyer and absented himself to make enquiries. The visitor was disappointed when Enriquez returned, not with a present-able young Frenchwoman, but the Dupont son and heir, Didier Marcel, who at once stiffened when he saw who the visitor was.

'Monsieur, I would have thought that you could spare us the pain brought about by your presence.'

Enriquez backed away, but stayed within hailing distance.

'Two of your recent guests have been murdered since we last came face to face, Didier, so do not presume that I have a lot of patience for the likes of you. Rowena Jane Randolph's death has upset me. I seek her employer, Mademoiselle Leduc, so as to find out more of the events leading up to Miss Randolph's demise. As it happens Mam'selle Leduc is on la Baronne's scheduled visiting list. Now, is she still with you?'

Didier stammered, but as he was being addressed in fluent French, a language unintelligible to the butler, his words could only be directed at his questioner.

'No, she is not here. Mam'selle Leduc was suffering from travel sickness part of the time she was with us. We had little to do with her. Most of her baggages remained packed, and she left several hours ago. Or was it yesterday? I really can't remember. What with all the work to do, and *maman's* indisposition, my memory is failing me.

'There was a private carriage, kept in readiness for the Leduc lady's departure. My parents thought that she had gone directly to the house known as the Dutch 'ouse. She has not been back. We do not expect her. I am sorry.'

'Is the Señorita Isabel still with you?'

'All of our guests have now departed, I am pleased to say. Adieu, monsieur.'

In order to score a point, Didier began to walk away.

Mike called: 'There is still the matter of Beauclerc artifacts, two of which I believe were stolen while in your house!'

Didier paused, inwardly seething. 'If I recall correctly, *you* were supposed to protect them, yourself!'

'But I was put out of the house at your request. You allowed a common policeman to manhandle me. How would you like to fight a duel, my brave

Monsieur Dupont? I am the affronted party, but you can have the choice of weapons! What do you say?'

Didier kept his face averted, breathing noisily. Mike chuckled.

'All right, you can relax, mon Didier. I will tell you one thing. It is unlikely that your nouveau riche bankers' family will ever set foot socially in the Chateau Beauclerc. Adieu.'

And so the two young men parted again. Mike at once felt that he had taken advantage of the young Dupont, but possibly other considerations of greater moment had made him act ungraciously. However, he had discovered one thing. Mademoiselle Leduc was almost as mysterious as Rowena Jane Randolph had been.

There was only one place for him to go to, if he followed up his fruitless search. The Dutch house. He found it some twenty minutes later, separated from Second Street South by a tall line of trees. Three people had answered his queries and helped him on his way.

A sympathetic landlady showed him into the room where Rowena Jane had died. He felt overcome by the knowledge, though he was only there for a few minutes. Although another person had used the room since Rowena's demise, a faint trace of her perfume still lingered in the wardrobe.

Before he went away again, the landlady assured him that no French mam'selle had been there to collect the English girl's property. What there was of it had been moved to the doctor's quarters, so she believed. Mike thought that very likely. Although he kept his feelings hidden as much as possible, the woman perceived the depth of his grief.

As he walked away, she called: 'I hope you get him, sir. The swine with the knife!'

Mike paused long enough to nod a couple of times, but words would not come. When he had ridden about one hundred yards, he began to gather his thoughts together. A slight detour took him to the telegraph office where a tired clerk had not long since finished composing and sending messages for Marshal van Dune.

'Anything for Liddell?'

'Where from, sir?'

Mike shrugged. 'Middleton, Sundown. Anywhere.'

'No, sir. Not this trip. Nothing at all.'

Mike felt like giving the fellow a tongue-lashing for prevaricating, but he kept control of himself and instead asked for a pad. As he received it, the palomino kicked the boards of the office sidewall. Mike made a mental note to see to the quadruped's needs next. It was only fair.

Slowly and deliberately, his mind on the situation at the other end, Mike composed his message.

To Madame la Baronne de Beauclerc, Sundown City. Mademoiselle Stephanie Louise Leduc attended Dupont reception Riverside. English girl companion died unnaturally in Riverside. Shun visitors. Stay put. Love. Leduc present whereabouts not known.

Mike Liddell.

Riverside.

Mike paid the rate for sending the message, intimated that he could probably be contacted through Doctor Bergerac, or the peace office, and then went away to see to the stabling of his tired mount.

He sat still in the saddle when a startled stroller heard him muttering and listened hard. The rider was saying:' *Don't you worry your head, ma'am. I'll get him . . .* '

13

At eleven o'clock the following morning, the streets of Sundown City, Sunset County's original settlement, were already beginning to reflect the heat and the time of the year. Shoppers were moving swiftly to finish their chores. Those shopkeepers who could afford a canvas awning for their windows were opening them, and the thirstiest of the community were wondering how much longer they would have to wait before showing an indecent haste to get to the nearest bar.

Jock McArthur, the town's veteran blacksmith, had worked for an hour and a half on a metal bracket of a special shape, intended to make a shelf in a corner of one of the Chateau Beauclerc's downstairs rooms.

Having finished the job, Jock wanted to be away from his forge and his tools for a while. Consequently, he had decided to deliver the article in question himself. He, therefore, exchanged a few words with his hard-working coloured striker and cleaned himself up for a visit.

Jock had no knowledge of foreign languages, but Madame la Baronne spoke excellent English quite effort-lessly, and she always made a fuss of the hirsute old man on his infrequent visits. Divested of his work overall and apron, he strolled off down the street in his shiny grey jacket and black Sunday stetson. Just as he was passing the telegraph office, the clerk looked out.

Kale, the clerk, was an angular fellow, all green eye-shade and thick spec-tacles, but at that time of the day his focusing was fairly good. Kale noticed what Jock had swinging from his left arm, and at once he deduced that only one household in the town would want a bracket like that. He darted across to his door, swung it open and called after the 'smith.

'Hey, Jock, good morning to you! Are you goin' anywhere special?'

Jock paused, his eyes hardening under his jutting grey brows. His private view of Kale was that the fellow pranced about like a monkey when he was behind the windows of his establishment. Altogether too nervy: too restless for a man in that sort of work.

'Mornin' Kale. If you're thinkin' of usin' me for a delivery boy, you can think again. I've got one callin' place, an' my time's limited.'

Kale grinned, showing yellow gapped teeth. 'In that case, you won't mind just handin' over a telegraph message to the lady at the chateau, will you? Could be worth a glass of wine to you, friend. Think of it!'

Jock, who still tended to colour up when offered hospitality at the chateau, simmered down and grudgingly accepted the folded piece of paper which Kale tucked into his jacket pocket. Jock's other hand appeared to be occupied by his big bowled tobacco pipe.

'I'll put a word in for you, Kale, it won't be a good one, though!'

Jock nodded, moved on again, and privately grinned at the clerk's momentary discomfiture. Five minutes later, he was approaching the front of the so-called chateau, a big stylish wooden building on the northern outskirts of town. His pipe was in his pocket now, warm but empty. He was whistling through his plump lips a tune used by his ancestors in Scotland for marching. A regular bagpiper's march.

A divan swing in the garden, hidden by a tall neatly trimmed hedge, stopped creaking. Madame la Baronne, who had been taking in the fresh air on the swing, stepped indoors and alerted the butler.

'Joseph, Mr McArthur is on his way to the front door. Be so good as to bring him through to the side gallery and produce some coffee for us.'

Joseph, a negro with silver hair, opened the front door and beamed at Jock. 'Good mornin' old friend. The mistress wants me to take you through to talk to her, an' I'm to get coffee, as well. Don't give me no trouble 'cause I ain't supposed to take no for an answer. All right?'

Jock beamed, gushed and removed his new black hat. On tiptoe, he followed Joseph through to the gallery in question and found Madeleine standing by a table and chairs, waiting for him.

Madeleine had a Japanese-style kimono wrapped around her light summer dress. Small dark-haired figurines on the back of it were in direct contrast to her own tall, shapely elegant figure and her long golden tresses carefully combed up on the back of her head.

'My dear Mr McArthur, you've stopped work specially to bring me the wall bracket, haven't you?'

Jock half bowed, shuffled a chair under his hostess, and produced the white sheet of paper which Kale had asked him to deliver. 'I wanted you to have it, ma'am, the moment it was finished. And this message, too, which the telegraph clerk asked me to deliver. I hope it is good news.'

Madeleine flushed a little and her hand trembled as she accepted the paper. Joseph appeared almost at the same time, and la Baronne instructed him to pour out and quench Jock's thirst while she stole a look at the message.

To Madame la Baronne de Beauclerc, Sundown City.

Mademoiselle Stephanie Louise Leduc attended Dupont reception at Riverside. Present whereabouts unknown. English girl companion died suddenly at Riverside. Shun visitors. Stay put.

Michael Liddell.

Riverside.

With an effort, Madeleine held in check her mounting discomfiture about the tone of the letter. She beamed at the blacksmith and her own man, Joseph.

'Joseph, I want to see you sitting here with Mr McArthur and passing the time of day with him. Entertain him a bit. Me, I am slightly indisposed. Forgive me.'

After bestowing upon each of them one of her warmest smiles, she moved into the house proper and located Mollie O'Callan in the kitchen. Mollie was combing out her long auburn tresses by the open outside door.

'What is it, Madame?'

'Read this, Mollie, and tell me what you think.' Madeleine slipped into an upright chair with a patterned cushion tied to it. Mollie read the message quickly and glanced over it a second time. 'Well?'

Mollie gave it back. She rested a hand gently on Madeleine's knee.

'Well, obviously Michael doesn't want us to stray too far away from the house. He seems to be in a suspicious mood, as this Leduc person appears to have gone off without leaving an address. Michael has to be suspicious to protect us. It's his way, you understand?'

'You don't think the English girl who died met with foul play, Mollie?' Madeline laid a hand delicately upon her throat.

Mollie could see the mounting panic in her mistress' expressive blue eyes. A kidnapping and various attempts at robbery had left her nerves in an uncertain state.

'It may be so, Madame, but we shall have to wait for further details. Mike has seen fit to inform us about the death, the presence in the district of the Leduc woman and so on. At the back of it all, I guess he really wanted to ask us once again if all is well. I wonder if he got to know her at all?'

Madeleine stood up and paced the floor. 'It isn't at all clear on that point, is it? But *I* know her! At least by repute. My late father-in-law, Monsieur le Comte, had several staunch friends when he left the old country. One of them was a certain Baron Leduc. In fact, le Comte brought to this country a valuable artifact belonging to Monsieur le Baron. I haven't seen it lately. It's a coronet. The letters of the Leduc name, L E D U C are worked into five upright pieces of precious metal, and the centre piece on the top is a rather large cut stone. A diamond, I think.'

Madeleine paused beside Mollie and gently stroked her long auborn tresses. They were more like sisters than mistress and companion.

'And how does Mademoiselle Leduc fit into the story?' Mollie queried, with the sudden enthusiasm of her Irish upbringing.

Madeleine relaxed, and stepped through the open door into the secluded back garden. Mollie, in a light work smock, joined her.

'There can't be two people of exactly the same name, can there, Mollie?'

'With a name like that, it is highly unlikely, I'd say. Why do you ask?'

'Because the Leduc coronet is mentioned

in le Comte's papers. According to the agreement made between le Comte and Baron Leduc, the coronet is to be collected from this house, either by Baron Leduc himself, or by his accredited heir, in this case his heiress. He has no surviving sons. Stephanie Louise Leduc is the heiress.

'Furthermore, the coronet becomes available to her on her thirtieth birthday, and I believe that may be this year. I don't know what I'd do without you, Mollie. We must both go through to the side gallery and make a fuss of Mr McArthur, who brought the message. After he's gone, I must go through le Comte's papers to check when Stephanie's thirtieth birthday is likely to be, and you can seek out the coronet and give it a polish. It'll be something for us to do, deep our minds off other considerations, like Mike not being here.'

Mollie smiled broadly, taking ten years off her normal serious expression and looking almost girlish in the process. 'I think I know exactly where the coronet is at this moment, Madeleine. It is under the false bottom in the box ottoman in your private dressing room!'

It was Madeleine's turn to laugh. Her mounting laughter sounded like the cadences of a trained operatic soprano.

'Ha, ha, in my dressing up box, of all places. We must try it on, in case we have to part with it shortly.'

Before they joined the men on the gallery, Madeleine turned serious for a moment. 'If Stephanie has really come to the States to collect the coronet, I think she might have written to me in advance, don't you?'

Mollie agreed with her, but made light of the point of etiquette so that Madeleine would not start brooding again.

★   ★   ★

'I wonder if Madeleine la Baronne de Beauclerc often goes away from her distinguished residence these days?'

The speaker was a woman in her late thirties, with a well rounded figure, short brown hair and long shapely legs. On this occasion, her feet were encased in mocassins. She wore no leg covering. She had on a flounced maroon skirt and an off the shoulder puckered blouse of a brighter red.

She and her two male companions were sharing a two-room board building which had once been situated south of Middleton and to the south-east of Riverside. After being abandoned by telegraph workers, it had been dismantled, uprooted and shifted to its present position in a remote valley considerably further north.

One of the main items in the room they were sharing was an old but firm barber's chair. In it lolled the long lean figure of a man in his middle thirties with a past connected with the French Foreign Legion and cavalry horses. His eroded bulbous eyes were closed. A small cresent-shaped duelling scar showed quite clearly just wide of his left eye.

The second man, who was much more on the alert, strolled about the cabin on silent feet, his thoughts mostly elsewhere, although he had his twin revolvers, his rifle and a long bladed knife spread out on the table, along with a cleaning cloth.

'If you are lookin' for an answer from your French friend, I can tell you he's dozed off to sleep again. Give a Frenchman a glass or two of wine, an' that's it. Until the sun does down.'

The woman giggled. 'Be careful, Rufus. He can loll about like that for hours an' never move a muscle. I've seen him do it. Seems I'm not going to get an answer to my question.'

Volk took the basin of warm water, the brush and the soap away from the woman, and dumped them on the corner of the table. At the same time, the woman removed a half smoked short cigar from between the finger and thumb of the drooping sleeper and put it between her full lips, drawing on it with obvious satisfaction. Her brooding brown eyes contemplated Volk, who had changed his rig recently and was now wearing an outfit of fringed grey buckskin.

'What do you say, Rufe? Do I shave him over the top of his head now, like he wanted, or do we put off the matter of changing our appearance until later in the day?'

'I say we get started,' Volk answered lightly. 'See here, I'll take a hand if you like. After all, if you want him to practise forging la Baronne's handwriting the sooner he starts practisin' the better. Watch me.'

No one knew better than Manuela how unpredictable Charles Guerin could be if anyone upset him or caught him unawares. However, this character, Volk, also had a formidable reputation. She drew back, leaned against an outer wall beside a window and simply watched. Volk hummed lightly to himself as he worked up a lather on the worn-down brush and gently applied it to the top of Guerin's crown.

Guerin started, blinked and closed his eyes again. He straightened his neck as if he was enjoying the sensation and spread his small tight mouth in a grin, accentuating his lantern jaw.

'*Ma vie*, that feels good, Manuela, you have the touch of a midwife. But I hope you remembered to sharpen my cutthroat razor before attempting a job such as this.'

In fact, the Frenchman's cranial hair and sideburns had lost their sleek beaverskin appearance some months ago. Now, it was nowhere longer than half an inch in length. He adjusted the towel so that it fitted more closely about his neck, protecting his collarless white shirt and the upper part of his stiff cavalry trousers.

From the window, Manuela murmured: 'Just keep still is all I ask, Charles. We can't afford to have accidents, eh?'

Guerin grunted and nodded slightly.

Volk, meanwhile, carried on with the lathering process and appeared to be getting progressively more satisfaction out of it. Manuela moved to the stove, taking with her a cloud of cigar smoke. She was in the process of warming some curling tongs, prior to working on a fine wig of blonde hair resting on a dummy head at the back of the table.

'Did you sharpen my razor?' Guerin asked again, sleepily.

'Of course I sharpened it,' the woman returned sharply. She was about to add something about Guerin cutting his own hair, but Volk's continued efforts prevented her.

Having finished the lathering process, Volk was about to pick up and test the razor, but some peculiar quirk in his unpredictable nature made him neglect the razor and pick up his belt knife instead. Laughing without sound, he tested the keeness of the blade on the end of his thumb, and then stepped close behind his client.

With Guerin's skull secured between

his chest and his left hand, he began the first careful strokes with the knife. He worked from the forehead up towards the crown. The excess loose hair and lather was wiped off on a cloth at the end of every stroke. Volk achieved a rhythm and Guerin accepted it.

Manuela got on with her curling, using a lot of natural dexterity. One long tress after another was rapidly wound up on the tongs, squeezed and secured with a strip of cloth.

The sides and back of Guerin's head responded with equal ease to the crown. Volk paused every so often, miming little messages to Manuela which made her want to laugh, but she dared not, in the circumstances.

Guerin hummed an old Legion marching song to himself, which he finally curtailed to make a comment. 'Do you two folks think it would be unlucky for me to set eyes on my new appearance before the razor has completed its work?'

'It might, at that, Charles, so be

patient,' Manuela suggested.

Guerin chuckled. 'The razor has never worked better, my girl, and your fingers are nice and firm, as usual, but you seem to be usin' a lot of pressure. Is it really necessary?'

Volk and the woman exchanged glaces. Manuela was nervous whereas the makeshift barber indicated that he was indifferent about the outcome.

'What's going on?' Guerin queried suspiciously.

'*Mon ami*, it is nothing. Except that the hand holding the cutter is not Manuela's. It is mine. So be still an' let me be finished. It won't take long.'

Guerin's eyelids flickered, but he did not open his eyes. He chuckled, maintained his rigid position, and rumbled inwardly with suppressed laughter. 'It seems, my little Manuela, that our new associate has other talents than the ones we know about. We must not underestimate him. Never underestimate an enemy, or a friend.'

A silence grew between them, which

eventually Volk broke by declaring that the head shaving was completed. He wiped the shiny bald skull, stepped back and handed another cloth to his client. Meanwhile, Manuela moved around and examined her lover and business partner with renewed interest. Guerin studied their two faces, and then moved over to a wall where a mirror was fixed.

'So, a new Guerin, quite different from the other one. I would have looked good like this in my legionnaire's uniform, wearing my kepi! I don't think many of our old enemies will recognise me like this. But hand me the razor, one of you, my jaw needs a bit of a scrape, too.'

The woman moved over to give him the razor. He toyed with it for a few moments as he soaped his chin. Eventually, he became aware that it had a certain dryness to it. His bulbous eyes focused on Volk.

'If you didn't use my razor, what *did* you use?'

Volk grinned broadly, toyed with his knife and held it up.

'Your belt knife, Volk! The one with which you terminated the English girl, Rowena Randolph. I say. When I think where it has been!'

He turned away, not certain whether he ought to feel repulsed. He began to scrape his chin with the razor, while Manuela stared at the knife blade as though hypnotised. Presently, Volk sheathed it and began to pick up his other weapons.

'What a fuss to make over one nice clean little knife. Anyways, I wouldn't have had to use it on the English girl if you hadn't allowed her to find out you weren't the real Leduc woman. You ought to get on with that wig business, an' make Charles, here, get started on one or two letters to Madame la Baronne.

'You have copies of her handwriting to copy from. If she won't come out without a special reason we must give her one. We know she's more or less expectin' a visit from the Leduc woman. All you've got to do is to decide where.

'That remote disused church you mentioned on the way here. West of Sundown you said it was. Where the recluse priest used to live. We can easily set up an ambush there.'

'What if she won't come out?' Manuela queried disconsolately.

'Then we'll think of something else. But we have to be positive about a future plan. I'll be back.'

So saying, Volk stepped out of the cabin. Within five minutes, he was engaged in target practice, working as if he was going in for a prestigious competition.

Manuela found herself wondering which of her men partners would prove the more effective when the showdown occurred.

14

A day later, Mike Liddell was in the township of Pecos Creek, an older settlement well to the east of Riverside, located at a spot where the creek waters were still formidable enough to require a small boat in which to cross over. Being well to the east of the significant river, Pecos Creek did not regularly attract much out of town traffic.

Mike had ridden to the new location because his enquiries in Riverside had failed to bear fruit. He rode along, goaded by uncertainty and the only thing he could be assured of was that his journeying was taking him in the direction of Sundown, where the Chateau Beauclerc was located and where his biggest responsibility lay.

If Sanchez, Guerin and Volk intended to launch an attack upon the chateau or any of its regular residents, then he was travelling in the right direction. Not knowing exactly where the enemies of the Beauclerc menage were located played havoc with his nerves.

As the town relaxed after the intense heat of noon and afternoon, the troubled young Texan began his enquiries. The constable manning the peace office knew of no significant strangers in town, or passing through. After drawing a blank in the obvious place, Mike wilted. He knew the enormity of his search for the three determined desperadoes. At times, he wondered if he would be justified in riding flat out for Sundown, putting all else aside in favour of strengthening the defences of the vulnerable household.

Now, as he strolled and questioned, he knew in his innermost thoughts that he was hoping for a showdown with the trio of enemies before la Baronne and her retainers had to be involved. For over an hour, he drifted into saloons, passed the time of day with shopkeepers opening up again after siesta closing, and chatting with strollers on the street.

Eventually, something drew him to a shop near the east end of town. There was a faded canvas sun blind protecting the window. On display were plaques, effigies, sacred ornaments: the establishment had a quiet remote aura about it. No food, no groceries, no souvenirs. Only high class goods for customers of refinement. Mike glanced up at the writing above the window. Apparently, the proprietor was an Italian; one who had been born in the holy city of Rome, Italy. Luigi Mattioli.

Mike tried the door, found it still locked and knocked gently on the glass panel. After a second knock, the dark blind behind the glass of the door was moved down slightly. A pair of recessed serious dark eyes regarded him over the top of it. The door key was turned and still the door was held on a chain.

'Good day, señor, what is the nature of your business?'

'Good day, señor. I would like to look

at some of your stock and to make a few enquiries of you. If I don't disturb you unduly.'

The shopkeeper appeared to consider the matter for a lengthy period, but eventually he opened the door, retreated behind the nearest counter and showcases, and meekly awaited further developments. After browsing for several minutes, Mike judged that the time was ripe for asking questions.

'Señor, you do not exhibit many paintings, but I wonder if you have ever been asked to purchase anything of that nature? I had in mind miniatures. My employer has a collection of such items, mostly painted in Holland.'

Mike would have said more, but already Mattioli had reacted rather emotionally. His breathing had deepened. He was a small person, lean and sallow complexioned. At fifty-five years of age his thinning dark hair was brushed back, straight and flat. He looked underweight in his grey smoking jacket.

'What is it, señor? You look disturbed. If there is anything I can do to help . . . '

Mattioli gradually relaxed again. He tattooed the counter with nervous fingers and contrived a makeshift smile.

'I was asked about miniature paintings only this morning and the stranger who asked me had a miniature silver salver which he wanted to dispose of. In fact, it was a genuine piece with the madonna and child upon it. But I don't have any sale value for such an item. So I declined. I suggested that there was a shop in Middleton where the salver could possibly be disposed of, but the enquirer was not inclined to take pleasure in the suggestion.

'In fact, he showed a remarkable change in temperament, in outlook. It was almost as if he had two personalities, one pleasant and the other evil. He became restless, and I felt oppressed until he settled his gaze upon that small range of vestments.'

He indicated items of an outfit which

a priest might wear, on occasion. They all appeared to be the same size, as if all the possible clients were of the same proportions. Mike studied the vestments more closely.

Mattioli shrugged. 'All of those are of the same size, to fit a small priest. In fact, one man only. El Padre Claudio. I keep them for Padre Claudio as a special favour. If I see him, or his sacristan, Felipe, once a year, I am lucky.'

'Did your customer wish to buy vestments?'

Mattioli nodded. 'I pointed out that they were all for a small man, that I only kept them in stock for one special person. My innocent words seemed to upset him even more. I felt menaced in my own shop, so I pleaded indisposition and retreated to my quarters at the rear. Had there been a rear entrance, I would have used it and called help, but I have only the one way in and out. So I stayed out of sight, and presently, when I looked he had gone.'

'Did he steal anything?'

'Yes, he did. Curiously enough, only a cassock, a gown and a few other things intended for Padre Claudio. I found the incident very disturbing. That was why I was so reluctant to admit you just now.'

Mattioli came out from behind the counter. He walked through to the rear, and gestured for Mike to accompany him. Seated on either side of a low table and sampling a glass of white wine, the two men continued to communicate. Mattioli did not know where his morning customer had come from or where he went to, but the meeting had made a vivid impression upon him.

'Can you tell me about the place where your Padre Claudio lives, señor?'

'I am not good at distances, but La Iglesia de la Torre, as the locals call his church, is north of the trail linking Pecos Creek with Sundown City. It is quite remote. The church and the padre's cottage are the only two permanent buildings, these days. The ordinary people who built the church, the tower and the priest's dwelling are no longer there.

'There was a landslide. It was all very sad. Their own homes were built of less durable materials. The shifting rock and soil flattened them. A few people were killed. In spite of their religion, they were superstitious and they feared it was a place of ill omen. So, they drifted away, seeking other places to live.

'After a time, only Felipe Perez, the sacristan, stayed on to look after el Padre. Felipe himself is probably nearing sixty-five years of age, and Padre Claudio is much older. Felipe is an expert gardener. He grows a lot of food. I haven't seen either of them for over a year, so I can't say if they are in good health. What else can I tell you, señor?'

Mike was listening well, but at the same time his imagination was racing along in parallel. He was intrigued to know that Padre Claudio's church and residence were so remote, and that they appeared to be within one half day's ride of Sundown City.

'It may be that I have to pay a call on Padre Claudio some time, señor. If I do, I will make sure he and his old sexton are in good health, rest assured. As to your earlier visitor, I think you were wise to stay out of his clutches. So far, you have not described his appearance. I am simply guessing who he might be. Perhaps if I described the man I have in mind?'

Mattioli poured a little more wine.

Mike began: 'Well, he has a slightly misshapen nose, a face well wrinkled for a man of forty. Swarthy complexion, I'd say. A small moustache the last time I saw him. His forehead is broad and low. His brows curled up. And his eyes are dark and restless. Hair dark and brushed across. He covers it with a flat-crowned grey stetson.'

Mattioli remained quite still, except for the beads of perspiration which appeared unbidden on his brow. As Mike paused, the shopkeeper nodded very definitely.

'Did you mention to him where the small priest lived, señor?'

The shopkeeper's brow furrowed. 'I don't think so, but I can't be sure. Is it important?'

'It may be,' Mike replied calmly. 'I think I may visit the priest quite soon. But I have taken up a lot of your time. Now, I must go. I don't think your unwanted customer will return, but you would be advised to keep on the watch. I will make sure the local peace office knows of the incident. Adios, señor.'

Mattioli showed him as far as the front door, and — in marked contrast to his earlier attitude — acted as if he was reluctant for his visitor to leave.

* * *

Fifteen minutes later, Mike bounded into the telegraph office in such a manner that the duty clerk upset his chess board and had to crawl under the counter to repossess two pawns. By the time he had righted the board and put all the pieces back on it in the starting position, Mike had scribbled over half a page of his message pad and made his alterations to the gist of the message.

The clerk pushed his spectacles up his forehead and squinted at the writing, which he read aloud. 'To Wagner, Middleton. Hoping to contact our friend at La Iglesia de la Torre north of Pecos Creek Sundown trail. Alert undertakers earliest. Greetings. Mike Liddell. Pecos Creek.'

'How much will it be, friend?'

The spectacles were lowered while Mike was inspected. The clerk quoted a figure. Mike explained to him that any delays could cost lives. The clerk moved to his apparatus, having taken possession of the money, reflected upon the matter of undertakers in the message, and decided that the 'sender' was probably quite serious. When next he looked up, Mike had departed.

★   ★   ★

Another day. Mollie O'Callan was moving lightly along a sidewalk in Sundown, in the middle of her morning shopping when a gruff voice called out to her from the batwing opening of a saloon which she had just passed. She paused, a basket on her arm, and licked her lips.

'Hey, Miss O'Callan, is that you?'

The voice was like a bullhorn croak. In fact, it belonged to one of the oldest inhabitants of Sundown, the saloon's owner, one Bluey Darwin who had been around when the first settlers put down their roots to found the town. He must have recounted the tale of the so-called city's beginnings a thousand times since the Sundowner saloon first opened to the public.

Darwin's back and legs had been giving him trouble for the last year or two, so that he was less mobile than he cared to be. Nevertheless, from his creaking wheelchair in its privileged position within the saloon, he still controlled a lot of conversation with his broad Australian accent and he continued to be a fine advertisement for the establishment's mediocre brew of beer.

Mollie rightly divined that Darwin would not be calling to her unless he had some message of importance. Old Bluey knew his place, and it was not with the personnel of the French house. Mollie pushed her basket further up her arm, shouldered her way through the batwings and adjusted her eyes to the gloom within.

Bluey moved his chair considerably nearer the door, and gestured for her to sit down at a vacant table. Mollie smiled and refused the offer of a drink, preferring to stick to business.

Bluey grinned. 'A fellow came through a few hours ago. Came from Pecos way, I think. He brought a letter with him. A gent asked him to deliver it to the Beauclerc residence. Not bein' used to big 'ouses, he got as far as the Sundowner an' asked me to send it the rest of the way. 'Ere it is. Over to you. I paid 'im a dollar for 'is trouble. 'Ope that was all right, Miss O'Callan?'

He gave her his big toothed, thin lipped grin and handed over the letter in question. It was crumpled, as far as the envelope was concerned, but it looked genuine enough. Mollie took a dollar from her purse, handed it over and began to open it.

As it was addressed to Madame la Baronne, Bluey showed surprise. He would have been more surprised if he could read Mollie's thoughts. If Bluey had given the messenger a half dollar instead of a dollar, she could have believed him more easily. The old Australian was notorious for being tight-fisted throughout the community.

The inside address surprised her, for a start. La Iglesia de la Torre. She had never visited the Iglesia de la Torre, but she had heard rumours about it. La Baronne occasionally sent gifts to the old priest and his sexton, who lived there. Mollie had to concentrate to understand the letter, which was written in French. She had never been taught the language in her Irish youth, but she had picked up a useful knowledge of it since taking up work in service.

She translated as she went along.

'Dear Madame la Baronne. You will be surprised to receive a letter from me when I have contrived to get within a few miles of your residence without having told you. Alas, since I came south to visit with the Duponts in Riverside, and your own self, I am afraid my health has gone back on me a little. Although I am very keen to see you and to enjoy your company for a while, I find myself rather limp and weary with travel sickness at the home of Padre Claudio but a few miles from Sundown.

'I bring you greetings from your cousin in Canada, but before I can give you them in person, I must take a few days rest with the good priest. However, he has said that if you should like to make the short journey on horseback to his home that you will be very welcome. I would dearly love to talk with you in this lovely rural setting, but if you too are prone to travel malaise I will understand. For the present, sincere greetings from your sincere friend, Stephanie Louise Leduc.'

Mollie blinked hard, looked up and stared at the old Australian without actually seeing him. 'And what do you think of that?' she remarked absently.

'Can't say I make anything of it at all, Miss Mollie, on account of I don't do a lot of close readin' these days. A matter of poor eyesight. I'm sure you'll understand. I *did* think it was addressed to the lady of the 'ouse, 'owever, but I'm sure *you* know best, eh?'

This time Mollie laughed, and took away the other's burning resentment. 'How long since it came into your hands, Bluey'

'Thirty minutes, or one hour, at the most.'

He was prepared to argue, but Mollie had run out of gossiping time and she showed it by rising to her feet and heading for the batwings, once more. She promised to tell la Baronne how helpful he had been. He nodded and blinked and she was gone. Only the swinging batwings were moving. He snorted, yawned and went about, heading for the bar and a fresh pint of lukewarm beer.

★　★　★

Mollie finished her chores in another ten minutes. As soon as she arrived at the barber's shop, the men's hairdresser pulled aside a curtain, ushered her through and called to his daughter who was in the quarters at the rear.

Lily Timpson was a plump Scottish brunette of twenty-seven years who still spoke with her native accent. She enjoyed a spell with Mollie every few weeks when the latter called in to have her long auburn tresses trimmed, washed and curled. But on this occasion, she could tell that Mollie was disturbed as soon as their eyes met.

'What is it, Mollie? Something wrong at the big house, is it?'

'I don't rightly know, Lily. But there could be trouble for la Baronne.' She slumped into the hairdressing chair, permitted Lily to put a clean towel round her shoulders and then accepted the habitual cup of coffee. 'If you don't mind, I'll ask you just to trim my hair this time. After that, I've got a big favour to ask.'

'Ask as soon as you're ready, Mollie. I'll not see you worried for the sake of a bit of friendly assistance. Is the coffee to your liking?'

Mollie sipped, drank rather more deeply and outlined what she had in mind. 'In a letter I've just collected, a strange French woman is tryin' to get la Baronne to ride out into the country, to La Iglesia de la Torre, to see her.

'It could be a genuine request, and then again it might not. Mike doesn't want any strange visitors while he's away, and there have been attempts in the past to lure Madeleine away from the house. So, what I propose to do is go and see for myself. If the offer is genuine, then I'll back Madeleine's right to go and visit. Otherwise, she'll stay where she is.'

Lily finished her own coffee, and reached for Mollie's cup.

'How do I fit in?'

'You can deliver the letter to the big house. Say, one hour after I've left. I propose to ride there, alone. After all, I've had enough ridin' practice since I took up this sort of work.'

Lily nodded, pursed her lips and smoothed down her overall over her generous bosom.

'I want to borrow your pony, your riding kit. That's how you fit in. Is it asking too much, Lily?'

'Not at all, not at all. I'll send somebody for the pony straight away.' She slipped into her father's part of the establishment, had words with a man just on the way out, and came back again. 'There, it'll be round the back in ten minutes, or so. I don't suppose there's anything we can chat about while I do the snipping?'

Assured of the assistance she needed, Mollie was able to relax and chat without effort. Lily fitted her out with a shirt, denims, boots and other accessories. Lily's riding boots were slightly loose on Mollie's feet, but otherwise their dimensions were very similar.

By eleven, Mollie was on her way: her long hair tied back in a ribbon, and her freckled face hidden by a turned down straw hat rim.

15

Towards one o'clock in the afternoon, Mollie started to approach the location of La Iglesia de la Torre through a thinning tree stand on the east side. Lily's lively pony had behaved well. Although it did not like unfamiliar riders it did nothing to unsaddle her.

By the time, her *derrière* had grown accustomed to the grooves in the saddle and the unfamiliar contours in the quadruped's back. Lily had insisted on her taking a gun belt, but Mollie — being unfamiliar with such hardware — felt it a drag on her waist.

Mollie did not expect that the Leduc woman would travel alone. Therefore, she was expecting to see four people. The Mam'selle Leduc, her companion, the priest and his sexton. Even as she was mulling over the possibilities on the downward track through the trees, it occurred to her that the chateau had already been informed about the female companion of Stephanie Louise Leduc. The English girl Mike had telegraphed about! The one who had died in Riverside. So, if the English girl was dead, who was escorting the Leduc woman? The mystery deepened.

As the last of the timber came in sight, she checked the pony and sat quite still, studying the distant vista. The church was a squat rectangular building, its stone camouflaged in places by patches of lichen. The tall tower, if Mollie had her bearings right, faced towards the north. In the upper part of its structure, four openings, one on each side, revealed an old discoloured bell. Mollie had never heard anyone say they had heard it being rung. The bell tower was narrower than the main structure. Added onto the sides of the tower were two extra rooms. The one on the near side was used as a vestry and the one on the other served as a base for the piano.

Some of the windows were large, and still had glass in them. Others were tall and narrow, almost as though put in for defence. The main entrance was to the south. A little to westward of the southern aspect the priest's stone cottage and a stable were under the same roof, shrouded in large old trees, resplendent in foliage.

Not too far away, there were human voices, arguing and teasing each other, while slightly further away a few horses and a mule cropped grass and swotted away flies with their tails. The voice of one human was female. With her full lips sucked in, Mollie counselled herself to be cautious. This was the critical time. She had made this long ride with one express purpose, to observe those who wanted la Baronne to ride out and meet them.

She dismounted, fixed her reins over a bush, slackened the saddle and gave the pony a friendly pat or two. It flashed its tail a time or two, having expected a drink and a proper rest, but there was

256

reasonable grass nearby and it soon settled down.

Mollie mopped herself down, checked that the revolver was in good order, and set off Indian fashion to study the priest's house and its surroundings. For the first part of the survey, the fringe of trees screened her, but after that she was ducking and crouching and sometimes squirming along like a tailless newt. In time, she made it round the back of the stone cottage; the knees of her denims were green with grass rubbing and her straw hat was stuck to her forehead. Inevitably, her excitement mounted.

The exchanges she had heard earlier were clearly not coming from the house. They were in the church. The bits she had overheard, however, did not sound like anyone involved in church business. The windows at the back of the house were streaked, as if they had not been cleaned for some time. She felt that something was not right. When she came up with the two burial mounds, some of her ideas began to clarify themselves.

One had been there longer than the other. Weeds in the soil made that clear. The name on the older headstone was that of Felipe Perez, the veteran sexton. The date suggested that he had been dead for more than six months. The information chipped out on the stone had been done with an unsteady hand, but it was legible. The soil of the other mound was rich and fresh. It had only been turned quite recently. The second headstone was a twin to the other, but so far no information had been added to it. Mollie was left in a puzzled frame of mind. Someone had died recently, but who? Common sense suggested the old priest, who was at least seventy-five. If Padre Claudio was dead, had he died a natural death, or had some unwanted visitor despatched him? Or was Mollie becoming altogether too melodramatic in her womanly deductions?

In spite of the discomfort caused by covert crawling about, she decided to keep her presence a secret from the other live humans for a short while longer.

Next, she had to find out who it was in the church, and what they were up to. Having decided, she moved away again, intent upon getting to the weathered outside door giving access to the vestry.

*　*　*

In the south-west corner of the church, Charles Guerin was strutting up and down in a curtained-off alcove in a white cassock. It fitted him well, except that his ankles showed beneath it, on account of the length of his legs. As he walked, he practised the flat-footed way of moving often adopted by tall clergy. At the same time, he manipulated a small skull cap, seeking the best place on his hairless cranium for its location.

Volk was happy to see him in his new rig-out, the one which he had brought along from Pecos Creek. 'I told you it would fit you, amigo. All you have to do to look respectable is have Manuela, here, lower the hem. She'll do that for you, an' then you'll look like a true man of God. Now, put your two hands together an' try to look pious.'

'I'd much rather la Baronne came here, so I don't have to play the part in public. But even so, if the cassock is lengthened it'll do, I suppose.'

Over at the north-east corner, the vestry door opened with a slight creak. Mollie entered, aware of the almost overpowering smell of damp and age in the stone and the woodwork of the disused room. She felt her heart would leap out of her chest as she tiptoed over to the inner door, and placed her ear to it.

As she did so, the woman's voice pealed out in laughter which had a raucous edge to it. The sort of laugh which a woman uses in men's company. Not a seductive laugh, but that of a member of a team, a committed conspirator. Now Mollie knew there was a conspiracy. Her first reaction was to get out, fast. However, having come a long distance to discover the true facts, she felt it unwise to withdraw without finding out more.

The voices of the conspirators were lowered. It was almost as if they knew there was an eavesdropper in the building. She made an effort to control her nerves. Not knowing how visible she would be when it opened, she tested the inner door, the one which gave access to the main building.

Volk was saying: 'I didn't enjoy buryin' the old priest. That's a habit I've never acquired, buryin' people. And now we have to come up with one which died a natural death goodness' knows how long ago, right at the outset of a lucrative showdown like this one. That cottage, I'm not sure if the odour has finally gone. And us expectin' a high-born visitor at any time!'

He groaned, produced his belt knife and cut into three a long cigar. For himself, he collected the longest end.

Manuela aimed for the other end, but she knew the meanness of Guerin and that made her leave the end and take the middle section. As the match rasped into light, there was a small noise somewhere down the nave. All three eyed each other, their faces close on account of the match.

Manuela blinked a few times. Guerin raised one eyebrow, the one near his old duelling scar, but Volk was entirely hooked on the sound. He mimed for the other two to keep on talking, while he sidefooted to the nearest curtain and looked out. His battered hat was hanging down the back of his neck by a thin cord. He put it back in its rightful place and kept on looking.

The draped altar was as it had always been. The choir stalls to left and right of it were still vacant, still dusty. So were the two lines of forms with their side and central aisles, set out in two serried ranks nearly all the way to the porch and the main entrance. And yet something had moved. Sanchez and

Guerin talked on, making a conversation about nothing. Volk turned his head from time to time, said 'Yer' or 'No' and still he watched.

At a critical moment, a mouse or a rat squeaked near the choir stalls on the east side. Mollie, who was hiding behind the altar, stifled a gasp and straightened up. Too late, she saw Volk's probing eyes on her. Because of the hidden rodent, she stayed away from the vestry door and instead sprang towards the door of the tower. She turned the handle and heaved it open, at once relieved that it *would* open, and quaking in case there was no exit into the open air.

It closed when she applied her weight, and suddenly she was in a compact, dark, claustrophobic atmosphere of beams, wooden stairs, cobwebs and squeaking rodents. Two small windows admitted daylight, but there was no way out. Progress had to be upwards. She tripped over a beam, and fell over others, heaped on the floor. By sheer good luck, a beam which she placed against the door fitted the space between the door itself and an upright prop supporting overhead timbers.

★ ★ ★

Volk said. 'A youngish woman with long auburn hair tied back. She slipped in on purpose and was trying to listen to our conversation. What do you make of her?'

Manuela used an unladylike word. 'Auburn hair, freckles, green eyes. The Irishwoman from the chateau. Mollie O'Callan! I wonder if there's anyone else with her?'

A quick examination of the out of doors, using the main door and a window suggested that the intruder was alone. Volk raced to the vestry, and he had the same impression.

'Leave her to me. She's safely in the tower, an' there's only one way out. You two, get yourselves on your way to the chateau. Be prepared to look for opportunities. Me, I'll deal with the colleen an' then I'll catch you up. Take your weapons, and don't forget that wig you did all the work on. It will put you in the same class as the French noble woman, I feel sure. *Vamos, vamos*! Get the horses an' high tails for Sundown, eh?'

Manuela nodded, glancing across to where Guerin was lifting up his cassock, prior to running out of doors. And then Volk had put them out of his mind. He danced down the church, sidestepped round the altar and confidently put his right shoulder to the door. His thoughts were on what he might achieve with a cringing redhead more than anything else. The firmness of the door gave his frame a jolt and put him in a bad mood.

He stood back and filled his lungs, thinking about frightening her into opening the door. Something made him not bother. Instead, he pulled his right hand .44 and put a bullet through the woodwork, where the lock ought to be.

The bullet went in all right, but the door remained just as secure as before.

In his second attack, he used a foot, but he was careful not to have his leg too stiff in case he did himself some real damage. Again, the door timbers were too strong for him. He backed off and used his lungs. No response.

In fact, he had to work for nearly twenty minutes, trying levers and then having recourse to an old rusty axe before he finally was able to get through the door and see what lay beyond. The dust made him cough, and while he was still incapacitated, a small unused bell came down from above, narrowly missing his head and making the pile of wooden beams rise up and fly in all directions.

He was reminded that persons with that colour of hair often have more than their fair share of spirit.

★   ★   ★

Mollie was terrified, but still thinking clearly. She was well above the danger

266

level when Volk broke through. The falling bell was a bonus. She had not meant to really aim it at him. It got out of control when she was attempting to shift it.

Three sections of zigzag wooden staircase connected the ground level with the underside of the so-called bell chamber, and at each level a makeshift wooden platform of planks formed a ceiling of sorts. Volk angrily fired a few shots upwards, through the different levels, but his efforts provoked no immediate response. Moving with care, he gradually climbed higher. At each level he fired a shot upwards, as though attempting to prey upon the nerves of his victim.

Directly under the bell chamber, he was grinning unseen when he fired three bullets upwards, aimed about a yard apart. As the echoes faded, he strained to hear any sort of giveaway sound. The reaction was totally unexpected. From up above, Mollie fired back three of her own. One of her bullets passed between Volk's hat brim and his cheekbone and that left him whistling soundlessly.

He was too close for hapless firing, and she surely had more bullets in her weapon. What other method did he have to be rid of her?

★   ★   ★

Bats had added to Mollie's listed fears. And yet she was not ready to give in. Perched as she was on a broad slab of stone dragged up there for the benefit of any workman engaged on repairs, she felt temporarily safe. Bullets through the floor would not harm her, hitting the underside of the slab.

Ten minutes later, she knew what to expect next. Volk had resorted to fire. The whole tower edifice seemed to be dry. And down below there was an excess of spare timber. Eddying smoke began to penetrate, travelling upwards . . .

Mollie began to cough. She wondered how much space she had above her in which to manoeuvre. There was just a loose-fitting trapdoor, and a long narrow gap in the woodwork through which a strip of leather went, on its way to the bell.

How well was the bell secured? She had heard tell of one old bell crashing all the way to the foot of the tower when a gale dislodged it.

Maybe the bell would work for her, make a big booming noise and attract attention from the right sort of people. It was worth trying. The thin shafts of light enabled her to see where the lower end of the leather strip was secured. She worked at the fastenings, succeeded in loosening it and then wondered if she had the strength to set the bell in motion. She gritted her teeth, gripped the metal handle attached to the strip and moved back along her stone perch. It needed an effort, but not as much as she had anticipated. In fact, she was hauling on the tongue, not the bell itself. Whoever had rung for a service must have had to use a lot of energy . . .

Walk with it as far as she dare, and then release the tension. She winced as the bell reacted when the tongue hit it. The sound it made suggested that there was a crack in the bell, but nevertheless it made a loud booming sound which affected her ears, giving her the impression that loud noise was part and parcel of her very being.

Husbanding her strength, and fighting the nausea of noise, she went through the exercise over and over again. Eventually, the smoke made her cough and her stamina went back upon her. Volk tried another two bullets, but he failed to distract her. Her coughing became worse. With it came the heat, and the promise of greater dangers still to come.

Mollie abandoned her bell ringing and half crawled up the narrow wooden steps to the trapdoor. Any sort of resistance and she felt she would have had to stop and cry, but it yielded quite quickly and she was through it and on the platform of the bell itself, with the openings on every side and a relieving breeze coming in at her to show that there was still another world beyond the tower of fire.

She had her wits about her, and yet she had to explore. To get at her, Volk had to come up through that same trapdoor, so she knew where to focus her attention. She licked her lips, checked that her revolver was to hand, and glanced out of the nearest opening, hoping to gain confidence through what she could see. The height took her by surprise, making her giddy.

Shaken again, she undid the borrowed hat, discarded it and untied her hair. Was it a forlorn hope that any friendly human might look up and notice her crowning glory?

16

La Iglesia de la Torre was due for more visitors than it had known since the local population moved away.

Mike Liddell was within four hundred yards of the church even before the cracked bell began to peal. Hearing it, he pushed his sweating mount to a greater effort, convincing himself that he had found the right place, and that some sort of a crisis was being enacted even as he approached.

He manoeuvred the palomino out of an arroyo and rode it in a spirited fashion along the fringe of stunted oaks, approaching from the south-west.

★　★　★

On an entirely different approach route across unbroken country from west-north-west came Earl Marden and his associates, the Bayer brothers. They had also ridden hard and purely by coincidence they were within half a mile when the clanging started. The smoke and the noise had the same effect upon this trio as it had upon the young Texan.

'Let's use a touch of the rowel, boys,' Earl advised. 'If you ask me, the church is on fire an' it's possible somebody could be trapped in there! *Vamos*!'

★　★　★

From a few points further to the north came another rider, a man with a bronzed skin: an Indian who only shunned the company of white men when he felt the need to use the element of surprise in serious matters. This was a serious matter. Johnnie Two Feathers began to piece together the evidence put before his senses, as he neared the scene of the confrontation. He, it was, who first glimpsed the swinging bell of auburn hair as the frightened woman danced around from one opening to another.

'Mollie O'Callan. Alone up there. Being smoked out, and frightened for her life. I wonder who is below, putting the pressure on?'

He acknowledged having done a white American trick, that of talking to himself. After that, he talked no more, but schooled himself for a silent approach. Not much more than instinct told him that others were on the move. He knew that there was a good chance the others were friends, but he was not taking any chances. Already, he had ascertained that the tower was not climbable on the outside without the aid of a rope. He had lariats with him, as always, but would the woman come down, terrified as she was, without anyone up top to support her?

★ ★ ★

Mike Liddell took in a whole lot of detail in the last fifty yards. Mollie. The

274

smoke. The way the girl was behaving. What sounded like an occasional bullet fired up the tower from within. He shouted hoarsely at his tiring mount, bullied it to its maximum speed and rode in close, along the side of the vestry and beyond. Nothing from the vestry door other than a slight hint of whirling smoke.

Mike knew an enemy held the nave of the church. In order to keep the element of surprise, he fired his Winchester through each of three windows down the east side, totally oblivious of the damage he was doing. At the corner, he turned the yellow horse, sent it past the main entrance, and leapt for the opened double doors.

After recovering his breath, he kicked open the inner door and rolled in his hat. A sudden fusillade of revolver shots picked it up and hurled it through the air. It would never be the same again. The shots were coming from down the seat area formally used by the congregation. Mike was hampered because he did not know the layout. He exchanged bullets on and off for a minute or two, and then decided that it would be too long and risky, getting in at the point. Most of the fire appeared to be still confined to the tower, too.

Instinct told him that only one man was in control of the church interior. He had a feeling that he was up against the elusive assassin, the bounty hunter, Rufus Volk. Time would tell, if he survived. Mike wriggled further towards the double doors, whistled loudly for the yellow horse and fired two Winchester bullets down the nave.

The frightened horse came, but reluctantly. The muscles of Mike's back stiffened with apprehension as he scrambled back into the saddle, but no lethal bullet sailed towards him. Mounted again, he turned the south-west corner and rode down the other side, pumping the occasional bullet through the glass of the windows. There was nothing of merit in what he was doing, but he had to keep his adversary thinking, if not guessing. For his own part, he had a theory of sorts about the vestry and the identical room on the opposite side of the tower. He was surmising that these two areas were, in fact, cut off from the main body of the church.

Having blasted three windows in a line, he discarded his beloved Winchester, steeled himself for reckless action and leapt from the saddle through the window of the smaller room. Even while the glass was still flying and his own body in the air, he knew that he had gambled and lost. There was no wall to screen the area he was landing in from the main part of the church.

Directly in his downward path was an upright piano. His flying boots slithered on the top of it. His bunched weight hit the lid of the top, and as he half somersaulted backwards the piano tilted under the impact and fell backwards. His twisting body, still falling, scraped the keys, as the other lid had been left open. His shoulders, his elbows and his gun belt punished the venerable keys and produced a short sharp crescendo of sound which soon faded off.

Dust filled the air. Inwardly, the piano sound sank to a dying boom. Bits of glass tinkled, still falling and the man's body was pitched towards the choir stalls on the near side. Mike somersaulted without being aware of it. The draped altar screened him from the earliest hostile bullets. Then began a duel of revolver bullets, the guns in the hands of two experts. Up and down, they stalked one another. No fired bullet was ever more than an inch or two away from its human target. From time to time, smoke made both men cough. The flying lead added new knot holes to the old worshippers' benches. A lot of lead was expended with neither getting the upper hand.

★   ★   ★

Outside, Johnnie Two Feathers had already turned his hand to the problem of Mollie at the top of the tower. By the time Earl and the Bayer brothers rode up, Johnnie had contrived to reach the roof of the vestry. He had with him two lariats, fastened together. In order to propel them upwards, he had attached a large stone and a sling arrangment. While he attempted to hurl the weighted end up and through one of the tower openings, one of the Bayers caught his runaway pinto pony, which he had used as a platform to get on the roof.

'There's a gun battle goin' on inside, Earl!' he called hoarsely. 'I figure just two men. Probably the assassin fellow and Mike Liddell. Keep a watch on the entrances, just in case Mike comes off second best. Maybe you ought to let Mike know there's help waitin' for him out here. I'm not sure if I can get Mollie, but it would help Mike to know we're tryin'.'

Indoors, more bullets punctuated the

slow roaring of burning timbers.

'All right, Johnnie. Take care, though,' Earl remarked, in his hoarse throaty voice. 'Sam, get round the north end. If there's a way in on that side, cover it. You know what to do! Rusty, I want you to stick around here. Make sure no hostile jasper gets out of that vestry door an' upsets our arrangements! Me, I'll get along to the main door an' try to communicate with Mike! Don't under-estimate the opposition. Here we go!'

Earl moved briskly along the east wall, under the shattered window. Hidden from his view, Johnnie hurled the weight end of the lariats up to bell tower level and had it glance off the stonework. When it dropped the first time, it almost shattered the vestry roof. A second time, he failed, but he was tireless and determined. A third time, he threw with the other arm, the one with which he was less practised. To his surprise and delight the sling and stone went through the opening and actually clanged against the side of the bell.

As Johnnie was breathless, Rusty shouted up instructions to Mollie.

'Hey, Mollie, will you fasten that end of the lariat to something secure? You get my meaning?' Rusty's voice was not the clearest for shouting instructions in difficult conditions. Both of the brothers sounded quite nasal when they attempted to shout in the open. Johnnie soon recovered his breath, and his voice was more incisive.

'Fix the end of the rope, Mollie, an' start climbin' down. I'll come up part way to help you, if it's necessary, but you ought to start out on your own!'

Mollie nodded and waved, but she was far from being confident about her own part in her escape. She had no head for heights. All right, there were friends down below, but to get down to them she had to make a perilous descent from a great height. And where on earth could she tie the lariat, in any case? When she had stopped shaking, her thoughts cleared. The only spot she could think of was the tongue of the bell. That was a distinct possibility. The way the lariat was draped, it ought to be safe. So she knelt beside the bell and went to work with her fingers. The tongue was stout enough, but did she have the strength to do a good job? She worked on it. And then she turned a couple of loops over her handiwork. This was possible because the flames had burned through the holding leather strip down below. Falling timbers, mostly burned through, jarred her nerves as she finished the job.

She backed away from the bell, running the lariat through her hands as if it were a lifeline. Through the side opening, she looked down and saw Rusty waving. On the roof itself, Johnnie had one leg braced against the side of the tower.

'Put your legs over first. Do it slowly. Have your boots against the stonework, and come down a hand at a time!'

Mollie nodded and tried to smile. Her jaw shook. She thought of all the things which had happened to her since she left the Bogside in old Ireland and came to this vast new country in the immigrant boat. This was a testing time. Would she come through?

She hoisted one booted leg over the side, rested her stomach in the opening and followed up with the other leg . . .

★　★　★

The inner door of the main entrance to the church was still ajar. Earl Marden wriggled his way through it and marvelled at the smell of bullets and burning wood in such a place of worship. He arrived at a time when the two gun duellists had paused, each making an effort to keep loaded and to outthink the other. For a minute, almost, Earl wondered if he had come too late. Was it possible that Mike had been taken out by Jan Wilden's assassin? It would not do to take such a view . . .

'Hey, Mike, can you hear me? We've got the church surrounded an' Mollie is bein' taken care of! We're with you, amigo!'

No one answered. Was it bad news? He had shifted his position after calling his message, because he believed that an alert enemy would have fired at him on the offchance of eliminating him. What did the continued silence mean? If Mike didn't want to give away his position by calling back, that was understandable.

In an effort to break the impasse, Earl rolled over and fired one bullet at a chandelier hanging above the altar. It clanged and shifted the great candle holder. Having done that, he backed off and wriggled away again. At the same time, Mike sprang onto the draped altar in a desperate attempt to catch his adversary unprepared. He caught a glimpse of Volk as the latter slipped further up the aisle on the east side.

Steadying his gun hand, he fired three bullets and then dropped down and behind the altar once again. The area around Volk was ominously still.

Mike stalked him, expecting a sudden whiplash attack at any moment, but Volk had stayed in the same place. When eventually Mike was close enough to see the outcome, Volk's eyes were still open and looking upwards. Death had sealed them in an open stare of surprise. The second bullet had struck him in the head.

★　★　★

Outside, Mollie glanced down and lost her nerve with her perilous journey only half completed. She screamed, lost her footing on the stonework due to the borrowed roomy boots and slithered down the rope with her palms burning. The increasing pain made her let go. She dropped, cannoned off Johnnie, slithered down the roof and dropped again. Mike, who had just staggered along, broke her fall and was flattened for his effort.

Slightly the worse for wear, Mike, Earl, Rusty and Mollie pulled themselves together. Sam Bayer joined them.

Five minutes later, a procession came down the ordinary approach track from the direction of Sundown. Manuela Sanchez and her partner, Charles Guerin, had run into superior numbers. Having received her message through the barber's daughter, Madame la Baronne had decided to go along to the suspect rendezvous at La Iglesia de la Torre.

She rode in her surrey with Joseph her butler holding the reins. Experience had made her travel with care. Consequently, Town Marshal Abel Smith had deputised no fewer than ten riders to go along as escort. It was the sight of this mounted escort which made the two conspirators forget their vicious intentions in favour of some superlative acting.

Manuela had kept up a delicate conversation in French, as they returned to the church. She truly believed that she was accepted by Madeleine as Stephanie Louise Leduc, and that her priest companion was accepted as a travelling companion and friend of the late Padre Claudio.

Mike, Earl, Mollie and the Bayers walked to meet the surrey, as soon as it cleared the trees. After suggesting a break for coffee in the priest's cottage, the pseudo French heiress and her ally stayed mounted until they were round the cottage and headed for the paddock.

Mike acted as spokesman. 'The church tower has been fired, as you can see, but we have all survived. Only minor injuries. Tell me, Madame, are you sure about Stephanie Louise Leduc and her clergyman friend?'

Many serious faces awaited her answer. Suddenly, Madeleine laughed. All her old gaiety seemed to be back with her. 'Alas, my dear friends, the real Mam'selle Leduc shares a family weakness, a *bec-del-lièvre*! This young female has no such affliction, I fear! And her clergyman friend has a small duelling scar near his left eye. We've met before.'

Madeleine's face turned bleak.

Mike translated. 'The Leduc girl has a *harelip*, Madeleine? Then Manuela Sanchez must be back in our midst. And Capitaine Charles Guerin is here, too. They're at the paddock. If you will stay here, we'll deal with them.' Mike snapped his fingers. Earl, Sam and Rusty reacted at once, moving cautiously around the small trim cottage, while Johnnie Two Feathers remained at the shaft horses' head.

'I believe they overheard you, Madeleine,' Johnnie murmured.

Within a minute, Mike and Earl confirmed that the two conspirators had ridden off at speed, instead of converging on the cottage.

'It's a job for the posse, Madame,' the Indian added.

Marshal Abel Smith moved stiff-legged into the saddle, anticipating la Baronne's word of command, but she surprised him and all her friends by standing up in the surrey.

'Let them go, *mes amis*, I have more important work for you. Instead of

288

hunting my enemies, I would like you to deal with the fire in the church. When the time comes, I will have La Iglesia de la Torre refurbished. We have been fortunate on this occasion, and that is my wish.'

Few of the riders relished fire-fighting, especially without proper equipment, but as la Baronne was paying generous wages for the day no one objected. While the fire-fighters toiled, Madeleine led her personnel and friends into the priest's house. The men smoked. Joseph provided simple refreshments. Madeleine, herself, saw to Mollie's bleeding palms.

Mike Liddell, troubleshooter extraordinary, slumped in a low chair like a limp rag doll, happy in the knowledge that Madeleine's family, his folks, had survived yet another security crisis. Later, his two requests were favourably received. One was to visit Federal Marshal Wilden, and help speed his recovery. The other was to have Rowena Jane Randolph's casket buried in the grounds of the Beauclerc house.